Harrell & Connells

Survival of the Unfits

Written By
Samuel Flicker

Clever Fox® Publishing
Chennai • Bangalore

“Harrell & Connells”

CLEVER FOX PUBLISHING
Chennai, India

Published by CLEVER FOX PUBLISHING 2026

ISBN: 978-93-7500-338-0

Book Cover by Samruddhi Shende
Illustration by Samruddhi Shende

1st edition 2026

Table of Contents

Preface

In a world increasingly driven by readily available information, a curious paradox has emerged: the very knowledge meant to empower us can sometimes lead us astray, particularly concerning our health. This story was born from an observation of our modern preoccupation with wellness, where self-diagnosis, fuelled by online searches and anecdotal evidence, has become as common as consulting professional medical advice. My hope is that this novel will serve as a gentle reminder to trust the wisdom of trained professionals when our bodies signal distress, urging us to seek proper care rather than relying solely on the vast ocean of open knowledge around us.

However, this novel is more than just a cautionary tale. A love story is woven into the narrative, intended to be heart-warming and humorous. The story explores the complexities of human connection and highlights the importance of kindness and consideration. This is especially true in a world where everyone faces their own challenges.

Life is rarely perfect. Everyone makes choices, sometimes choosing peace, and sometimes choosing chaos. Most of us are simply doing our best with the circumstances we are given. Perhaps in this evolving world, the greatest strength lies not in flawlessness, but in empathy and support. It is hoped that the reader will find joy, reflection, and inspiration within the pages.

Introduction

Harrell & Connells: A Philosophical Romantic Journey of Self-Discovery and Second Chances.

Harrell believed her life was written in stone: happily married to her love, Jade, until the end. But a challenging health condition forces her to question everything. Convinced she is a burden, not a responsibility, she makes the heartbreaking decision to end her marriage and retreat to her quiet village, determined to reclaim control and build a life of independence through her small bakery.

In her pursuit of self-actualization, she reconnects with Dr. Connells, a familiar face from her past she had never truly "seen" before. Connells, long habituated to his comfortable, lonely existence, is drawn to Harrell's bravery and considerate nature. As he helps her understand her health, their shared vulnerability sparks an undeniable attraction. In a world where love often demands sacrifice, Harrell must confront a new philosophical dilemma: Can she allow herself a second chance at happiness, not just for love, but to find her own inner peace?

Through the lens of Harrell and Connells' journey, and the vibrant lives of the people of Pallena village, this Philosophical Romantic Fiction proves that peace is the one objective every person ultimately chooses.

Chapter 1

Happy Life slowly departing...

The ring of the bell echoed in the house; Harrell walked toward the door despite her familiar headache and stuffy nose. She opened the door with a forced smile, "Welcome Honey, how was work?" The Man with dark brown dead eyes walked in, wearing untidy clothes, complaining about his work. He placed grocery bags on the dining table while slumping into a chair.

.Jade Stone, Harrell's husband is a professional lawyer working under a very dignified law firm, where he had been steadily employed for four years, with a handsome salary and peaceful house along with a sweet home loan in the city "Thown".

Listening to her husband complaining, Harrell quietly smiles to herself, thinking how simple he was. She put the tea on the stove and sat facing Jade.

While she unpacked the groceries, Harrell suddenly sneezed, and her eyebrows started to kiss each other as the pain appeared in her stuffy nose. Jade concerned, asked her, if the cold was still there. She said "Ah! I am tired of this now. Every time we go to doctor, he says it is due to weather change, but this cold is just going back and forth, it's been five weeks now". Jade says "I think you got sinusitis. I know a doctor who can help us with this; I will make an appointment this week. We will go together. You need to take constant care of yourself, stay away from water and cold air for a while."

Really? I have to do the entire chores; obviously I need to touch the water. How will I take a bath without water? She stands with the posture of a perfect wife and brewed the tea for them. As they drink their tea, conversations slowly fades away, leaving a settled silence between them. They were both tired. Just a dinner and then bed, this marked as the closing of the day.

It had been four months now; Harrell was still suffering from the discomfort of a lingering cold. She is cautious, so she kept her distance from Jade, thinking it would be better for him to stay far far away from her snotty disease. When few actions can be repeated quite a few times and people start to get comfortable, those actions quietly become habits.

Jade was sympathetic, he watched Harrell toss and turn, a soft, congested sigh escaping her lips in middle of nights with her relentless sinus problem. It's been months now, the constant headaches from work weighed on him. When he comes home, he finds his wife is asleep on the couch with a half-finished plate of meal beside her. He stood over there for a moment of silence. He wanted to comfort her, but instead, he left her in the couch and went to freshen up.

Harrell woke up to the clink noise coming from the kitchen. Her eyes meet with dark brown eyes with warm smile. "Wakey, Wakey, dinner is ready. Let's have some soup and rice. You seem to be sleeping so well, I couldn't wake you up."

Finally, after a long time, Harrell and Jade had a peaceful dinner at their house. She knew this past 6 months were hard for them. The home they decide to make is now only a house where they eat, sleep and talk. The romance has been fading away. She takes every bite with new resolution that she will try to make her marriage a happy, warm and comforting for both of them.

The next day, Harrell wake up in the morning with clean nose and start preparing breakfast and lunchbox for her handsome Jade. She goes to bedroom with cup of tea and places it on the side table. Slowly whispering to Jade's ear, "Good Morning Honey. There's tea waiting for you," and walked back to kitchen. Jade woke up to a quite different morning; he took a moment to look around. He held the cup and drank his tea quietly. He watches her wife through the half-opened door from the bed, humming to herself and beating the egg. This is it; it is heaven for him. This is all he wanted.

Jade had met Harrell in the small town named "Pallena", where his grandma lived. During the summer vacation of final year of his college, he decided to visit her grandma. Harrell was the daughter of famous Baker of the Town, Emmanuelle Serene. They owned the Shop named "The Serene Bakers". He met her when her grandma was buying Banana Bread from their shop. Harrell was sitting on the counter with a pen tucked behind her ears, looking at him with her shy smile. He knew right away, she might be the girl of his dream.

Jade asked Harrell out for coffee. As the dates went well, feeling began to grow. Her innocent smile and his brave heart, two strangers, became locked in those summer dairies, writing a beautiful love story.

After three years of sweet, honest relationship, Jade finally gathered courage and proposed Harrell. They were married in Pallena's small church, and it has been eleven months to that joyous day.

While Jade was drowning in the memories of their past, love began to gather once more in their small space.

And then, suddenly. Harrell Sneezed! Jade just looked at her.

Maybe a little differently this time.

Jade heads to work, Harrell walked to the door with his lunchbox. She said she has prepared his special egg fried rice. Jade took the lunchbox and found Harrell looking into his eyes.

A sweet moment. Jade smiled, she leaned closer. He patted her hair and said he would be back soon.

Jade left without a kiss, once again.

And she stayed in the house, with silent embarrassment.

Another day with less and less romance.

Harrell said softly "Jade, it seems our **happy life slowly departing**"

Chapter 2

Can this ending will lead to my new beginning?

Harrell's sinuses had become like a heavy stone, slowly drowning their marriage into the deep, empty ocean of darkness.

Initially, Jade was very caring and sympathetic towards her. He'd suggest many remedies from warm tea and soups, yoga and Nasal spray, warm steam and herbal medicines but those actions made Harrell felt like she is a stray cat on the wet street, alone. Sometimes, the same situation is seen very differently through two pairs of eyes. One just wanted to be nice; they were being kind. And the other, who was struggling deeply while holding on to their pride felt as if they were being pitied.

Kindness can look like a pity from the other side.

Kindness is often given without expectation; yet you cannot control how others are thinking. An act of kindness by one can be received as a gesture of pity by another.

That's why I believe that being considerate is slightly better than being kind. Don't be kind merely to appear as a bigger person; be considerate instead. Don't make someone feel smaller. Especially in this world we are living in, where many walks around with a pocket of ego or self-respect.

You can never know, even a warm smile can hurt someone deeply.

One night, Jade was very late. Harrell was tired of waiting so she decided to take a walk in the corridor. When she walked past her floor to the stair case, she found Jade sitting alone on the stair alone looking on the ground with a cigar in his hand.

She wanted to confront him, but she couldn't. She is well aware about the silent distress between them. Her hesitation was the proof that the distance is wider than the distant between few stairs. She walked back to her apartment and went straight to bed.

When the time past a little, Jade comes to his apartment and opens the door with his own spare key, without even knocking as if he knew that she will be asleep by now.

He tiptoed into the bedroom after changing into his night suit. He slides himself in one side of the bed and his head hit the pillow, after 2 minutes a rhythm of snoring filled the room. Harrell still couldn't get a blink of sleep, even when her eyes were closed.

The morning came with dark heavy clouds; the rain was light but feeling was heavier.

Harrell was sitting on the couch. Jade sits beside her. She says that when she went to doctor, he declared that this sinus is a sub-acute sinusitis, they suggested going for medical treatment if still no improvement, then I might have to go for surgery. Jade said "That is good news finally we caught held of the problem, but why they still want give a medication, isn't it more than 6 months." To which Harrell replied "because my cold is back and forth. Doctor thinks it might be due to some allergies or may be genetic. He even prescribed Anti-Histamine pills."

"Yes, but this medication is making you drowsy every day that is what I am worried about the most. Is it possible if they can perform some minor surgery?" Jade said.

"Maybe you want me get treated as quickly as possible so you can start making love to me. Now I am all snotty, must be really hard for you to look at my disgusting face". She said without even looking at him.

Jade was shocked by the sudden implication.

The only sound in the room was the clock, hanging on the wall with a blank face.

The couple was tired and frustrated; this love is now turned to snotty situation.

Jade took a breath and said "Listen the reason I did not made a move on you because when this all started you said you don't want me to get sick. But before I knew it becomes a..."

"A habit", Harrell finally looked at him with sleepless eyes and says "Now I am just an unattractive person to you, along with this annoying disease."

Jade says, "please dear, I understand that you are frustrated because of constant headache, cough, sneezes, but is hard for me too. I have a job and it is not just simple paperwork, it involves a lots of investigation, research, being proactive all the time. I am having constant headache every day. Did you ever see me complaining about them to you?"

Harrell says, "You used to complain me about your work problem but not now. Now whenever we talk, it is just about taking rest taking medicine, do that, do this. Don't to this, don't do that. I can help you with your problem if you have anything to tell me. I am you wife, may be you have forgotten about me and only remembered my sinus."

Jade says, "You're always tired, Harrell," he'd sighed, his voice laced with unspoken disappointment. "It's like I'm living with a dull girl who is always tired, numb, and silent, you have stopped talking to me even when I get home. You just don't want to have conversation with me."

Harrell burst, "Why would I have conversation with a Man, who is constantly reminding me that I am patient? I need to take warm steam, drink warm tea, wear warm clothes, take medicine, take inhaler and then take medicine again and then go to sleep.... rest for a while.

I am tired, but with your constant nagging.

I know you really care about me, but..."

Harrell sighed and decides to end the conversation there. Maybe she was afraid of his answers.

"I am going to take a nap now. I feel very sleepy"

"Do you want me to make breakfast for you", Jade replied with concerned eyes. Harrell held his hand preciously and say "No, you can eat the toast and egg, it's on the table. I am sorry; I really need to rest,"

Harrell went to bed leaving frustrated Jade on his weekend.

The snotty nose, a perpetual pressure in her sinuses and feeling drowsy all the time due to high intake of medicines. She'd wake up feeling as if she hadn't slept, the constant battle for clear breathing leaves her fatigued and irritable.

She was not taking care of herself properly. For her, the battle with this cold was less important than the cold distant she is receiving from her husband. She was craving for hugs, cuddles, and a warm touch.

Her negative mind was dancing with uneventful scenarios.

On the other hand, Jade, with his patient heart, tried to understand the situation. He knew she is not feeling well from inside, being a woman is hard but if you get sick even now and then, this might lead to depression. He'd offer her warm compresses and endless cups of herbal tea. He'd research remedies and accompany her to countless doctors' appointments. He'd even, for a while, switched to unscented toiletries and cooking with less aromatic spices to accommodate her dulled senses. Yet, the distance between them grew.

Harrell felt like a burden on her husband instead of helping him. He is giving more important to her than his job. He used to get scolded by his superiors for taking frequent leave to accompany her to doctor. She regretted her word, she thought if she hasn't said those, may be Jade wouldn't be so involved in helping her. She wanted to go back to those silent distances. At least those times, the moments were just cold distant rather than feeling guilty.

Jade even though he is tired, but he was doing everything required to be better husband.

Harrell has stopped questioning about the love fading. She knows more than anybody else how lucky she got to have Jade as her husband. She also knows his skills and qualification. She was becoming a hindrance in his progress. He is very ambitious man but now his priority is to ensure his life partner gets all the attention and care she needed right now.

Harrell is looking at bigger picture. It is now one and half years of marriage. Where she couldn't be a good wife to Jade, who is now a perfect husband. The doctor recommended another doctor, who was a specialist in Sinusitis. To which Harrell just nodded but she knew she not going to another town as her husband has a job here in Thown and soon he will takeover his father's law firm in the near future. After overhearing a few calls between her husband and his superior, she realised that Jade might be considering the suggestion made by doctor.

Jade enters the living room, look at Harrell, she is peeling garlic on dining table. He walks toward her and says, "Do you want to go somewhere for a change?" Harrell smile slightly, "Yes, I want to go to my mother to Pallena".

"Great, should we go by next week, then" Jade says.

Harrell look at Jade with her firm eyes, "I want to go there alone and also I want go back as a daughter not as a wife".

Jade asks, "What do you mean?"

Harrell says, "I understand the situation we are now. I am suffering from a cold from more than 8 months, which comes and goes as it feels like. I know you are great husband. You have stood beside me firmly but I don't want to be person that holds you back. When we met for the first time, I loved your patience and intelligence. The fact you are studying to become a lawyer was very different from the people around me. You were the city boy and I was village girl. But regardless of situation you have given me respect. I feel like I getting better but I need a different place to restart. I don't want you to leave your 4 years of job for 13 months of marriage. I don't want to be kind to you, nor do I want you to be kind to me. So, tell me within this last 8 month we couldn't kiss, will you be able to make a child with me even if this sinus is not permanently fixed".

Jade says If required, we can go forward with surgery; it will help us move forward.

"What about the embarrassment locked in my memories? When I ask for kisses with just gestures, you left the house with few pats on my head. Do you think I am naïve? Tell me how you really feel about me. Every time I am sick, you have taken care of chores, groceries, taken leave from your job and accompanied me to hospital. The expenses you have to pay for my medicines and treatments. Also, there is no guarantee, will this be fixed if we meet the other doctors. Do you really want to work this around?"

Jade holds her hand, "I want to work everything out. I have promised to be with you and will be going to take every step needed to make you happy."

Harrell smiles and say "Maybe you have not realised but from last 3-4 month you always say that your head hurts, you are taking Pain Reliever every 2-3 days. Tell me, are you really okay? I can that see you are cutting off work and taking leaves. When we met you told me your dream is be a great lawyer like your father and mother. But I think you want leave your dream, health, your family traditions behind just to help your wife.

Listen, the feeling I had for you is different now, it used to be all love and care, but now it is more respect and care with a slight less love. A man so brilliant stayed beside me within this last 8 month in this weird odds' sickly situation.

But at the same time, you need to understand. I feel like I just becoming a reason of hardship for the man I respect and love the most. I want to you to grow, not to go down because of me. You have ambition and it not like you father and mother forced you to become a lawyer. In future, you might lead your Grandma's Firm and will replace your father as a chairman.

Do you think a person like me will look good beside you? A person who constantly needs help, medication and sleeps most of the time."

Jade replies, "I never said you are burdening me. It is not you who give me headache; it happens to lot of people who work like me."

Harrell says "Really, then when we were dating why you never complain about work so much, you used brag about how great you were at your work. The headaches started from last 3-4 months. Am I right?".

Jade replies by turning his eyes down "Yes I never used to have these headaches before".

Harrell says, "Yes, I think, it is due to overwork. For me, you want to go to doctor and get all the prescribed medicines but for yourself you will take medicines without any prescription. Why?

You tell me take care about my health and give all around world remedies. And when I ask to go see a doctor, you shut me up saying it is just slight pain nothing severe. You can take care of me, but you don't want to listen to my word about you and your health".

Jade says, "What are trying to say, that I have not given you importance?"

Harrell replies, "No, I am not saying that, I am saying you are very surprised by my sudden question about intimacy and to cover that you have put a lot more effort toward me, which is making you feel exhausted and me feel guilty. I know I have stupidly made some bad implication on you. But you need to see we are becoming the reason of letting each other down. I am just saying, this marriage will be really hard if we want to go like this till the end. Do you want be in this hard marriage or not?"

Jade firmly says "Yes I want; I promised you that I going to give a better life"

Harrell straighten and says "That was a wedding ceremony and a marriage cannot just go on to fulfil a vow of being with each other in every sickness and wellness. It is more about supporting your life partner and making them happy, comfortable and safe. You do make me feel safe, but now I am unhappy and uncomfortable. Not your fault though. I have only one life, I cannot live this life being a burden on someone who I know is more capable of living much better life without me. I want to live with less guilt. I cannot be reason of your hard time. I don't want you to sacrifice anymore. I don't have guts to live my life in shadow of kindness.

I want to free.

So…

Give me divorce".

Jade understood what Harrell was implying. Yes, he was unhappy. He was tired. He was questioning everything. He knew she is not wrong, but is she really right.

Did one year and one month really deserve to end like this? Was it justified? There were no raised voices, no accusations; there was a mutual acknowledgment of efforts. The couple realized that while love seemingly fading and respect only remained, the life they wanted to share was no longer attainable together. To cling to this marriage has brought more quiet sorrow than joy. It might be the time to let go.

The air they once struggled to breathe together cleared a pathway for them to find the space to see their truest selves; now, it allows them to finally breathe freely, even if it means being apart.

A divorce happened leaving Jade and Harrell walking in different directions.

The beautiful scenery becomes past; the places were ruined; they never tried to hold together. Now they have lost themselves.

Harrell looks at the tickets and says to herself, "**Can this ending will lead to my new beginning?**"

Chapter 3

Take a deep breath, give yourself some rest!!

The familiar scent of rising dough, sweet cinnamon, and burnt sugar filled Harrell's nostrils the moment she stepped back into Pallena, her village. It was the scent of her childhood, a comforting embrace that contrasted sharply with the bitter taste the divorce had left in her mouth.

Her mother, Veronica, a formidable woman with flour perpetually dusting her apron, simply nodded as Harrell entered the small, bustling bakery. There was no questioning, no tearful reunion – just the steady rhythm of kneading, shaping, and baking, a rhythm Harrell instinctively fell back into. She started by washing dishes, and then graduated to glazing pastries, her hands slowly remembering the motions.

The village was much the same: cows wandered idly down cobblestone streets, children chased each other through fields of golden wheat, and the old banyan tree still stood guard over the village square. But Harrell felt different. The scars of her failed marriage lingered, whispered in the lonely nights spent in her childhood bedroom.

The next afternoon, while delivering a freshly baked wedding cake to a nearby home, Harrell overheard snippets of conversation: "Harrell, the divorcee, back in Pallena now." The words stung, but she held her head high. She realized then that the healing wouldn't happen overnight, but she knew her steps are in right direction.

She started spending her mornings helping her mom with the bakery's accounts, applying her sharp business skills she'd honed in her previous life. In the afternoons, she silently stayed in her bedroom muted by her unhappy marriage.

Days passed, and she felt like a broken leaf drifting in the wind, finding a place to stay still. She was sad, disappointed, and burdened by shame. She gets irritated by the cheerful laughs of the children living in her home.

Diana and Ron, the two kids were back from their school. They are cousins of Harrell and children of her mother's sister July. July and her husband David moved in with Veronica to support their bakery when Harrell got married.

Harrell was the second child. She has an elder brother named Liam Serene. Liam Serene is Professor who is married to his beautiful colleague, Professor Maria and moved to neighbour town, Watsar.

Harrell was sitting beside window, looking at her small yet peaceful village. A tear fell, hand stayed still on her laps. She knew she has to walk out of that place which is slowly breaking her. And she was trying but she is broken inside. When she was discussing the divorce with her mother, her mother asked not to give up. But she didn't listen to her and now she is not able to look straight to her mother's eyes. Yes, she was trying to run away from all the confrontation.

"Just a sickness that's it, this is why you both want to get apart. Is marriage a joke for both of you? Do you have any idea how I and your father stood with each other in every situation. When your father at his death bed, suffering throughout his last days. I stayed beside him, I knew and he also knew that nothing will going to change. But we still smiled and comforted each other in every possible way. And you want to go away from him, because of just 8 months of hardship. I raised you better than this."

Harrell with heavy heart, teary eyes looked at mother in front of court, "Mom, I know marriage is tough and I failed. You were the woman who stayed strong beside the father and build our bakery. You stood with pride; I am standing here with embarrassment, tired of this occasional sickness. He was making effort to make me better but I could only see him sacrificing his time, his job, his dream. I want to live free, not to be problem of others. I can take care of myself".

Veronica knows her daughter is not a fool; she must have gone through something very hard otherwise a big decision like this will not occur. She stayed beside her daughter through all the procedure.

"Harrell, come to shop, Susanne and Vivi is waiting for you", her mother voice echo in bakery home.

"Oh my God, I was shocked when we heard the news, seriously you kicked him out of your life, what did he do? I knew my cousin was goody good guy and just a a little selfish when it comes to his Priorities" sarcasm made by Susanne Stone, Jade's Cousin.

Finally, a little change in Harrell faces, with an eyebrow judging Susanne with every possible way. "Nothing like that happen", Harrell says while sitting on the empty chair of her Serene Bakery.

Vivi Parker took Harrell's Hand, looked with her most innocence eyes "I am here for you, you can shout at me, yell at me, tell me everything". Susanne whisper, "Isn't yell and shout mean the same thing".

The chatter chatter started, with so much updates, this trio of Pallena has finally reunited. Vivi shares about her morning trouble with her third pregnancy and how her husband Louise has successfully expanded their poultry with their new bird family addition, Turkey and Geese. Susanne shared her daily boring life in post office, following the same routine. But now she found another prey. Victor Tucker a new man force joined the Post Office, Pallena B.O. She has become quite friendly with him and help him is showing the place around. Harrell understood the situation, doesn't need more words. Both are happy and living there best life without any regret.

Harrell finally exploded and bombarded her friends with her marriage failure in every little detail; she could take out from her deepest dark and even cried through the conversations.

The afternoon left with yellowish evening on the windows of the bakery. The trio decided to end their meeting and going back to place they have to be. Vivi and Susanne waved back to the Harrell, who stood on the door with new, soft, pleasant smile.

It is very weird how old friend who don't stay in contact with you all the time, but when they meet, there is no grudges, only laughter, understanding and a deep sense of belonging. These people are like precious break that everyone needs to take from everyday routine, a necessity to keep moving on without giving up on yourself.

Harrell stood there watching the yellow-red-orange sky turning into pink-purple-blue. She felt a hand on her shoulder; she looked back and meets the serene eyes of her mother.

Veronica, seeing the flicker of hope in Harrell's eyes, handed her a small recipe book, it's pages yellowed with age. "Your Father's recipes," she said. "He always believed in new beginnings, like you do."

Harrell say "you called them here, don't you?"

"Yes, I know my child far better than anybody else. The path you have chosen is really hard. I do not agree with your decision but I am very proud of you for leaving the place that make you go down and have courage to start again from the beginning. I do understand that sometime some people can make you feel low, you cannot change anything there.

If you travel to different places, you can find your place where you can rise and shine without compromising others happiness, without being a burden."

Harrell hugged her mom, hardest.

Harrell flipped through the book, a smile slowly spreading across her face. Perhaps Pallena was not a place to hide from the past, but a place to embrace the future, a future baked with the sweetness of her father's forgotten recipes and the unwavering love of her mother.

A new beginning has been started, a story ended and a story began. A person with scars is now heading toward healing; it's going to take time. But it's okay. You are trying. That is what matter the most.

Veronica says "I am here. **Take a deep breath, give yourself some rest**."

Chapter 4

Now I am learning to hold on to myself

"One banana bread and one loaf bread, the total is eight euros, thank you… Have a nice day", Harrell said with a smile to the customer while sitting behind the counter of her bakery. She takes out a book and entered the amount in her journal.

July her aunt walks out of the kitchen and places a dozen croissant on the tray. "Do you want to taste one dear; your mom just took this out of the oven." Harrell took the offer and placed a croissant on a tissue paper. Sitting on the counter she bit the chunk of bread, "Oh god, ohm… so hot so hot, its straight out of oven!".

The door opened to a not-so-morning person. Susanne walked in, "Harrell, do you want to go out today evening? Just us. No men, no drama."

"Had a fight with Victor? Here, have some croissants" Harrell handed her half of her Croissant.

"Oh god, so hot so hot, it's really hot. So, you are coming or not", Susanne said impatiently. Harrell asked where she plans to go. Susanne says to the Kimsons. The woman dashing out the door.

"Kimsons", a voice came with a woman wearing an apron, with flour placed themselves like a cat cuddling to her owners, Veronica, Harrell's Mom walks in, "Are you going to Kimsons today?"

"Yes, I think so", Harrell said, surprised by her own answer.

"Great, me and July will also join you today, I will tell July." Veronica goes back leaving Harrell with her rapidly cooling croissants.

"Hmm!! walk fast ladies", Susanne barking down the street, storming ahead until she stops on the front of door with engraved "The Kimsons". She opens the door to Heritage of Pallena, a bar with an old-world charm, yet remarkably spotless.

One by one, ladies paved their way in. Harrell followed by Vivi, Veronica, July, Sara, Diana, Ruby and Maria.

Harrell sat at the bar with Susanne and Vivi. "Why are you so angry, you said no men, you didn't said anything about women. Also, I didn't say a word, they invited themselves".

"No, I am not angry; I am just a little frustrated. When I invited you, I thought even if Vivi come, still I will be hot one tonight, but why your brother's wife, the Professor Maria is here" Susanne whispered slowly.

"Hey, what do mean by that" Vivi said.

Veronica, with her sister July, and Sara her neighbour and best friend sat on one table.

Diana, Ruby sits beside Maria on the other table.

"Hey Debby, 7 beer and 2 hot chocolate for these two young girls here", Veronica said to the lady, sitting behind the bar counter.

This night is shimmered with flickering stars; the window with golden light coming out has distinguished rhythm of female voices, taking out their frustration with very sip of beer.

"Girls, why the dull face, is everything going alright in school" Maria asks Diana and Ruby. "Everything is fine" the girl silently nods with every sip of their hot chocolate. Maria with her keen eyes looks at them, "Really, there is nothing special going on".

"Leave them Maria, the both girls are little surprised with new changes, especially Ruby" Sara speaks with spirit of yawning.

Susanne looks at the Diana and Ruby and say "Girls always carry extras wherever you go, no one will ever help you, especially when you are most desperate. This is completely normal and natural thing. It can be a bit confusing at first, but no worries, you will get used the pain. Just don't scratch…

"Really! Such a topic of conversation in public? Some things are best to be kept private!" July says with firm face toward Susanne.

"I wish someone has told me that", Debby the bar owner states.

"Me too", Maria says.

"Yeah! Me too" Vivi with drowsy eyes and Harrell nodding beside her.

"Yep, must to know, this is things need to generalised" Veronica words shot from her eyes with warm smile, made July a little surprise but assured.

Suddenly the door shut open. A heavily bearded man, sporting a hat and clutching a small suitcase, appeared at the doorstep. He walks in making all the women all alert.

Looking at the faces of all the ladies, he knew, he is misunderstood.

"Oh! Son finally, you are here. Hey Veronica, you were asking about Connells yesterday and see he come." Debby walks to her son with a tight hug.

Veronica looks at him and says "You are really growing into bear. Are all the researchers and scientist required to grow bear to show that they working really hard."

"Yep, we just need to do and they pay us salary every end of month, in addition, it really scares the heck out of people, no thieves and burglar come near" Connells replied with tipping the hat.

"Connells, how many are they." Harrell whispers to Vivi and Susanne. "Did you know that Debby had a son?" Harrell asked to both of them. They both nodded. Susanne says "he is 4 years older than us and he is a doctor and very single. Oh wait!! Hey Connells, meet my friend Harrell. I told you about her last time".

Harrell alarmed by her best friend's action, she thought that Susanne might be wanted to come here, so that she can meet with this beard Doctor Guy with a plural name.

With quick beat of silence, Harrell looks toward the beard man.

"Oh! Hello Harrell, heard a lot about you from Susanne, I will be here for couple more days, if you have time, please do visit me. I would be eagerly waiting for you" Connells says to Harrell, as he goes inside the house by the door across the bar.

Harrell in her awkwardness take the last drop of the beer.

As unplanned night out ended, everyone walked in different direction to their homes. July, Maria and Diana were ahead of Harrell and Veronica as they were heading back.

Veronica looks toward her daughter, under the silence night with flickering stars. She felt as if Harrell is walking a different path in her mind. She is there but not seems to be present. Harrell eyes were trying to find something here and there.

"What Happened?" Veronica asks.

Harrell looks as her mom, "Nothing, just a little awkward back there. The way Susanne introduced me. Originally the plan was only me and her tonight. And I am thinking what she might have told him about me. And he even asked me to meet, in front of everyone. What is he even thinking? Does he even know I am Divorcee".

"Honey, everyone knows that here, it's a small village and people talk. But it's been a year. I don't think anyone care anymore. And if you want you can move on. I mean eventually you are young, beautiful so why don't you try? May be this time it will work." Veronica suggested her daughter.

"You know about my sinus problem right. Even though the cold has not appeared from weeks now, but still these kinds of problem are not cured, they stay with you forever." Harrell says, giving her a small hug as cold wind flew between them.

"One day I was frying some potatoes in the kitchen. I was bit clumsy back then. The wok with hot oil fell down and some of the hot oil splashed on my leg. I got burn. Emmanuelle came after hearing my loud voice. He shouted at me yet carried me to the doctor immediately. The burn was healed but scar remained. But it didn't matter to him, though he always follows me to the kitchen if I need to cook some fries. That is how life works.

Your body might get hurt; you might get sick. There will be scars. We will never be healthy all the time. Changes are inevitable. We need to accept the fact we cannot be perfect and no one will." Veronica's words of advice flows with wind away without touching Harrell.

"Yeah, you got lucky; it was just a scar not disease with snot. You no idea how I felt so disgusted. Even Jade eventually stopped kissing me and hugging me. Just a pat, is the entire warm I felt in ending of our Marriage." Harrell said to her mom as her nose was getting itchy.

Veronica says "I didn't know that was reason. Were you so stubborn to get divorced because of..."

"Achoo!!

Yes, rejection, loneliness, and losing my self-esteem. I felt disgusted." Harrell spoke with tired, timid voice. "But that are past and now I am living for myself and my people who care and respect me."

Harrell held her mother's hand. Their eyes met, steady and proud.

Harrell said, "Now **I am learning to hold on to myself.**"

Chapter 5

It was my fault.

Moisture hung heavy in the air; The land was wet. Wind rushed against the window of the wooden house in the middle of Pallena. Inside the room, a women put her foot on the floor, her hair unkempt, her eyes heavy with exhaustion.

"I am really tired today, can I just rest" Harrell said as she walked into the kitchen, removing the loaves from the oven and placing them on the table. The mother noticed Harrell is rubbing her eyes and her nose already running.

"Are you okay?" The baker questioned.

"It was raining in the morning, my sinus problem again." A sneeze erupted leaving her breathless with watering eyes.

She knew it would be a day of constant wiping and sniffling, the soft rhythm of rain returning outside, mocking her discomfort. It was a familiar ritual from the past year and a half that she'd grown to accept with a sigh, but never truly welcome. As she sits on the dining table.

"Here, has some tea" July put a cup of warm tea in front of Harrell and gives other to Veronica.

The three women sipped their tea on the cloudy morning. "Last night was fun", July's word fills the room with memories of last night. "Why don't you meet Connells today, tell him about your cold problem. He is doctor, he can help" July says to Harrell who is not delighted to hear.

Veronica asks July to take the bread to the bakery shop to the front. July stood and walks with tray of freshly baked bread that is ready to sell.

"About last night, I was thinking a lot and I understood the decision you made was act of self-esteem. I do get why you don't want to relationship anymore.

But dear I want you to know that the world is wider if you want to try new thing, want to meet new people. At the same time this world will become small, if you are meant to meet the destined one. Just do not make yourself the victim of the situation.

It's good to be hero, if you do not lose your things. But it's better to be a villain, if you have self-desires. Just do not break any rules and don't hurt anyone. But keep going on". Veronica speaks trying to motivate her daughter to have a desire of having Life partner so she does not have to see her daughter sufferings.

"So, you think Susanne is right to hitch me to that bear doctor with plural name" Harrell smirking through her red nose.

"You know his father, Mark Kimson, was the one who delivered you in this very house. Back then, our home was much smaller. Connells used to follow his dad all the time. At the time of the delivery, he was waiting outside with Liam. Liam was a bit older than Connells.

When you were born, they both come and looked at you, Liam was fierce he started jumping "My little sister, yeah!" and Connells was silent, he just stood there with smile.

He is kind Man. His father Mark was only doctor in our little village. He was there for anyone who needed his help. Kimson Family was famous for their small bar. But Mark was different from his family. He was interested in Herbal medicines. He left this village to study the same and came back as a doctor. He cured many people's illness and was the hero of our town.

Connells followed the path of her father, he went for "Doctor of Medicine". He is quite famous in this field. If Suzanne was planning this, I am really grateful toward her. Why don't you try? Try to meet him once, give yourself a chance."

Harrell says while she goes back to her room "Then this afternoon, I will go to Kimsons to meet him, since he was one who invited me."

The mighty Sun started to go down to the west after his daily habits of standing at the top at his supreme.

The girl was walking toward Kimsons wearing orange dress with sling bag. She opens the door finding the Man with clean face talking to an old lady. She walks in toward the owner Debby and ask her "Is Connells-s is still here. He said he wanted to meet me here yesterday". To which Debby replies "Right over there dear, checking-up with Granny Rosei.

All the olds have been marched to this bar from morning one after the other. He will be most probably free, wait for some time."

Here at the Serene Bakery, Susanne slams open the door finding Veronica on the Counter, "Is Harrell in her room".

"No, she went Kimsons today, thanks to your intervention." Veronica winked at her.

"Well, I had to; I cannot see Harrell suffering like this anymore. She is very nice. I want her to move out of this situation of "I cannot be loved by anyone"".

"Thank you dear, Harrell really need to start again, she cannot live her life all alone" Veronica offered mini banana bread to Susanne.

"Yeah, and Connells is really famous doctor, even his photo comes in newspaper many times." Susanne eating as well as showering bread crumbs on the table.

Veronica asks "What you told Connells about Harrell?"

"I told him, she did not have any cold like this before marriage but when she returned from Thown, suddenly she sneezes, especially when she is near any water or when it rains. I begged him a lot to help her; he is nice man he agreed. But I did not know that he will come back yesterday.

Thank God! We were there at that time, isn't it?" Susanne replies.

"So, you asked Harrell to meet Connells to get her sinus treated." Veronica question Susanne again.

"Yes, then what else will I ask him, he only doctor in our village. I mean why Harrell even travel to Watsar for treatment every month. Connells come here every 2-3 weeks. Why waste money?"

"Oh! Boy, women really make lots of baseless assumptions." words spurting out of worried Mom

"Eh!"

In Kimsons, the black-haired man escorting the charming old lady out with a gesture so warm, making him one of the kindest and the most popular in the village Pallena, Dr. Connells Kimsons.

Dr, Connells walks to the Bar and sat beside Harrell, "So, how are you?"

"I am good; did you have your lunch?" Harrell says, putting her string of hair to the back of her ear.

"Yep, before Granny Rosei came. So, tell me about yourself"

"Well, I am currently working with my mom on our bakery. I got divorced last year, and now I just focusing on expanding our business to neighbouring towns. Restricted myself from Dating Life for the time being… But I think now I can move on. You know if you meet new people, there might be a chance to meet the person, who is the destined one". Harrell nervously spoke, under the gaze of Connells.

"Wow! Hmm that sounds amazing. Now tell me about your sinus problem. I need every detail about..." Connells says while he cut off by slightly irritated lady.

"Why do you call my sinus a problem now? I though Susanne informed you about all. And weren't you the one who called me here yesterday, isn't it?" Harrell with worried expression looks toward the Man with one eyebrow reaching out to his hair, as if the eyebrow wanted to climb-up to his head.

"Understood woman, why angry? I need more history on your sinus infection so that I could provide the best consultation here. I don't like to make any mistake" Dr. Connells trying to explain the Lady here.

"But why?" Harrell asked.

"Hmm... Well, I am doctor and it is my job. That is what I do. Susanne said you visited some clinic in the Watsar, but still, you are not making much improvement." Dr Connells justified.

"Oh! Okay, so... I got this sinus the year before last, in August" and me and ex-husband went to doctor who gave me pills. After divorce when I come back to Pallena, last year in April, I started to go to the clinic of Watsar, who are also giving me pills but a little different once. Whenever my pills are finished, I go to clinic again." Harrell explained.

"Hmm... great! Could you do me a favour and elaborate your symptoms more? So that we could pick the root cause of your illness." Dr Connells said while opening his journal.

"Well, I got cold and we went to doctor, it was better when I took the pills. Once the effect of medicines is gone the cold come back again and again. I told Jade, my ex-husband and he told it might be sinus issue. So, we went to doctor" Harrell who was trying to remembering the memories. To which Dr. Connells specified, "Did you went and told the doctor that you have sinusitis or you told overall symptoms you were having at the time and doctor concluded that it is sinusitis.

"No, my ex-husband told the doctor that I have sinusitis" Harrell clarified.

"Is your husband a doctor, what was his specialization" Dr Connells, trying to seek more information as he already knew that Jade Stone was a Lawyer as Susanne was very angry when she was describing her cousin.

"No, my Ex-husband was Lawyer"

"Then how come he knows that you have sinusitis".

"I don't know, he was the one who used to talk to Doctors" Harrell look down, thinking did I really let that happen? Was I really under confident back then?

"Understood, so will you able to tell how it was started, what did you do that you got the cold and what kind of medicines you took. Has doctor ever tried to change you prescribed medicines or made some judgement. Any specific place you visit before you get watery nose?" Dr. Connells who was trying to get hold of information he needed.

Harrell was taken back, she pauses for a moment and look at him and says "I don't really remember how it was started but what I know whenever it rain or I get near water I sneeze and I don't take the medicine or proper care, the cold gets worse."

Dr. Connells ask, if she has any prescription or medicine with her. To which she replies, "I always carry them with me, here" Harrell hand over 3-4 types of Medicines

Dr. Connells check the medicines, "Hmm…, Azithromycin, Doxycycline these are Antibiotics, a Pain reliever and Antihistamines, which one of this you take often".

"I take Antihistamines mostly as Doctor told me take this whenever I get watery nose." Harrell says.

"What about the Pain, does it really hurt when you get the cold?" Dr Connells ask Harrell about more symptoms. "Well usually I get sneezes and then my nose gets watery. I don't feel that much pain, it gets better when I rest".

"Do you feel any facial pain or headaches, when you get cold or your nose gets itchy, I mean stuffy, feels like there is something is ticking in your Nose".

"Yes, I do feel itchy some time in here", Harrell point to her nose.

"Okay understood, do you have any allergies?" Dr Connells asked while noting down in his Journal. "I am allergic to Woollen clothes." Harrell specify.

Dr. Connells ask again, “Does you get any kind of specific rashes”, Harrell say “yes, the skin where woollen come in contact it becomes red and it itches a lot.”

“Does it worsen when you eat cold Curd or yogurt” Dr. Connells, look at Harrell taping the pen on the table.

“Sometimes” Harrell herself is wondering. Dr. Connells ask “That “Sometimes” you get rashes or hives or runny nose from curd”.

“Runny Nose” Harrell speak with confidence. “Okay so it is not a cold arthritis, but I can’t confirm it is sinusitis, it might be acute sinusitis.” Dr. Connells speak while looking for something.

“Does your face hurt when you get this cold, like here” Dr. Connells show with his hands under the eyes, cheeks, and forehead. Harrell says “No”.

“Then this is not sinusitis problem, you have some allergies, it might be “Hay Fever” or you can also say Allergic rhinitis. Your body overreacts to something in the air, like pollen, dust mites, Allergens, or pet dander or animal hair, which triggers cold-like symptoms such as a runny nose, sneezing, and itchy eyes. And after you take some Anti-histamine, you feel better.” Dr. Connells explains to Harrell.

“You mean I don’t have sinus” Harrell trying to reconfirm.

Dr Connells says, “Yes, it’s common for people to mistake allergic rhinitis I mean Hay Fever for sinusitis because they share some overlapping symptoms. But the causes and treatments differ. Allergic rhinitis is an allergic reaction in the nasal passages, while sinusitis involves inflammation of the sinus cavities. But you should know that the sometimes the allergic rhinitis can lead to sinusitis if the care is not taken correctly."

Harrell was listening to Connells and every word made Harrell how can she lead this happen. Where was her presence of mind? Just because Jade said it was Sinusitis, I did not even dare to confirm myself. Was I always so depended on Jade? I even changed the Doctor but all I informed next doctor that I have Sinusitis. And slowly she started to drown deep into her thought.

Suddenly, the bright sky from window was just scenery, the air inside feels like dark and heavy. Connells being a stranger & doctor, he understood that Harrell is now in the Jungle of her memories looking at the old rotten tree which is not even alive anymore.

"Sometimes we think that midnights are dark scary nights, but surprisingly in our mind we have fact fit in, it is 00.00 AM. That means something new is going to start" Connells word brought Harrell's eyes come to reality.

She looks at him. He says, "Was your previous husband very dominant? He looks a little selfish to me. How can he come to conclusion like that? Did he divorce you for this illness?"

Harrell smiled at Connells. The Smile was wise. Harrell was using her ultimate jewellery like all women uses when they know that they can't be understood.

Harrell says, "Dr. Connells, I think I knew all along… **it was my fault**".

Chapter 6

This is how we live. We are Social Animal.

The Mid-afternoon at the Kimsons Pub, the two strangers were finally becoming acquaintance.

Dr. Connells says "Harrell, I cannot agree or disagree was it your fault or not as I don't how you have been living up till now. But as a Doctor, I would say, its good thing that we are able to spot the cause of your problem. But I need further detail, so you need to keep your mind open and observe the changes in your body, the symptoms and the signs. What were you doing and where you were, when you get your nose watery and you start sneezing? I said it is Hay Fever on the basis of information you have provided me now."

Harrell says, "Sure, I will keep that in mind. But now what, I have been taking Anti-histamine wherever I get this cold and I do feel better after sometime. Do I need to do something else?"

"You can use different approaches like you can build your body more immune to the coldness, keeping things around you cleaner like your mattress, curtain, and clothes. Try to close the windows. Stay away from animal or pets. Ah… do you have pets?" Dr. Connells asked.

"No"

"Hmm, so tell me do you want the same allopathic approach or Herbal medicines would be better." Dr. Connells asked.

"I do know about three Healthcare ways, one is Allopathy, other is homeopathy and third one is Ayurveda, but what are Herbal medicines, is it different than Ayurvedic treatment?" Harrell asks.

Dr Connells explains, "Originally healthcare offers diverse approaches homeopathy, allopathy, and Ayurveda. Ayurveda is an ancient Indian system which focuses on balancing mind, body, and spirit using natural remedies which include Herbal Medicines, diet, and change in lifestyle for treatment including Yoga and Meditation. And Homeopathy is different but safe, its effectiveness is debated, it is "like cures like", uses diluted substances, it is slower but it cures the illness completely, while allopathy is modern medicine utilizes drugs, surgery, and diagnostics to target and treat diseases, it excels in emergencies and acute conditions but can have side effects on your body. So, choosing the right system depends on individual needs and the nature of the ailment."

Harrell asks, "Aren't you Doctor of Medicines, is it all the types or only Allopathic?"

Dr. Connells specify "Oh, I am part of Allopathic treatment, my father was Ayurvedic Doctor, he used herbal medicines to treat people."

"What do you think will be good for me?" Harrell asks again.

"Hm... What would be best is hard to say, everyone has a different body, so I cannot give justice on this recommendation, you were using Allopathic medicines up till now. Well, I cannot say it is not minimizing your allergies, but now-a-days, people are most widely using Allopathic system of medicine and it is widely accepted globally, and it has its own set of advantages and disadvantages. Allopathic is effective in treating serious and life-threatening diseases. It is backed by scientific research and is approved by regulatory bodies too. But you need to know this that Allopathic treats only the symptoms and not the underlying causes of diseases. These are very expensive, especially in developed countries like ours. And it relies on symptoms, correct diagnosis, tests and if only your body is able to accept the treatment or not. Allopathic medicines can have side effects and can be toxic in some cases. It makes you drowsy. They are chemicals simply so it will affect your body somehow, good and bad, depends."

Harrell say "If I want to use your father's approach, will it cure my cold completely".

"My father was doctor of Ayurveda, he used to tell me that if we want to prevent and want to have a holistic well-being, we have to take our body, mind, routine and surroundings into considerations. Well, I thing that Ayurveda is more suitable for chronic conditions. And if you want you can try some of it's approached to make yourself more Immune to your allergies. Like changing you routine, schedules, nasal Steam, mind control exercise like meditation and it is best if you start doing some Yoga, especially breathing exercises." Dr Connells suggest.

Harrell confirm "You mean I should do some morning exercises. I usually feels very tired in the morning, especially when I my nose gets watery, I feels feverish after sometime if I don't feel warm."

Dr Connells say "why don't you take some warm water or some tea after you wake up, it will increase the heat in your bodies. Have you ever heard of Kadha?

"No"

"It is special kind of tea, you need to take 2 glasses of water and add spices & herbs like black pepper, cloves, carom seeds, turmeric, Tulsi leaves, mint leaves, lemon, ginger, some even add garlic. You need to let it boil until the half of water remains. It increases heat in your body" Dr Connells explaining the Harrell on making Ancient Kadha of India. He adds "But you need to drink a lot of water after you take this Kadha as it might cause acidity, digestion issue, boils, difficulty in Urination, sometime bleeding from nose. You can try you can make this in your home, don't add the things that doesn't suit you."

Harrell say "Will it really help? You just said Herbal treatment do not have any side effect, but aren't this side effect. What about Homeopathy treatment?

Dr Connells "See, Homeopathy has been used for over 200 years and is popular among people looking for natural remedies. Homeopathy uses natural substances, which makes it safe and non-toxic. It treats the whole person, not just the symptoms. And the medicines are easy to administer and do not cause any side effects. But it is not effective in treating serious or life-threatening diseases. It can be time-consuming as it requires frequent consultations and follow-ups. Also, one should know that it is not backed by scientific evidence and is considered a pseudoscience by many people. But I see there are many clinics with Homeopathy treatment around. If want you can consult a Homeopathic Doctor, but the problem here is it is not an illness for you, it is your allergies."

Harrell says, "Then what can I do to make sure I am completely cure my illness" Harrell asks.

Dr Connells tap his right hand finger on the table like waves "Harrell listen to me carefully; you need to understand a thing about your condition. It is not an illness or a disease that will be cured, it is an allergic reaction due to some external particle that your body is not able to accept and it is causing a reaction. Your nose is become snotty. If you don't take any treatment. It will slowly give a head ache and fever. If you take some allergic medicines like Anti-histamine, then your body will start try to reduce these symptoms, but until the medicine is working. So, you need to focus on making your core stronger, improve your immunity, increase your stamina, make your body healthier."

Harrell get anxious "It will never be going to get cured, why this thing happened to me only? Why my body become like this, it was not like this when I was in this village?"

Meanwhile Connells stood up, went to the rack, poured some wine in a glass and drank "One day, a child caught a cold, he came to my father and my father gave him some medicine. Later, that same night, he collapsed. His parents, his uncle, and my father rushed him to the hospital in Watsar. When he was admitted and the doctor said that because of severe coughing, he wasn't able to breathe properly, and that he needed to put on a ventilator. With his father's consent, they put him on the ventilator. He started breathing. But only for few minutes, the coughing worsened, his lungs filled completely, and then he died"

Connells looked at Harrell with dead eyes.

"He died on the very same he caught the cold."

Harrell said "Why did he die?"

Dr. Connells said "He had asthma; the cold he got was swine flu. When the doctors put him on the ventilator, due to some uncalled condition the cough increased and filled his lungs completely, which ultimately led to his death.

There are many types of disease which look like a common cold but turn out to be something else. The cold you get is Allergic Rhinitis; it is different from Cold Rhinitis or Cold Allergy and completely different from Sinusitis.

Now, tell me, what choice did the doctors have? if he didn't put the kid on the ventilator, he would have died due to suffocation and since they put on the ventilator, the cold air increased the coughing in his lungs, which ultimately became the reason of his death. What could have been done here?"

Harrell sat still, staring into his eyes. There was silence, but seems like the question that had been asked has already been answered.

"That day, I understood when my friend Signalle died, Doctors are not God, they are ordinary humans like everyone else. On the basis of information the patient gives, they might identify the illness, but if not cured, the patient needs to go back to the same doctor and explain their symptoms clearly. The doctor might ask the patient to do further tests to try to find the cause of the illness. And when the problem is caught then the treatment will work.

That is what we say in our field that the job of doctor is to use their knowledge, experience and skill to correctly diagnose illness, decide on treatment and if required perform necessary procedures that will help the patient to recover."

Dr Connells finished his glass of wine and poured another. "You know what is the scariest part? he added. Even well-experienced doctors are still not sure if their treatment will work one-hundred percentage or not."

Harrell says "But we trust the doctors when they tell what medicines to take."

Dr Connells walked slowly and sat in his chair, "Does a patient really trust their doctor?"

Harrell eyes held a mysterious spark; she smiled gently and placed her hand on the table.

"Will you help me Dr. Connells?"

A little surprised but a more amazed, Connells smiled back.

"Mind my words young lady, I am quite charming, don't fall for me."

"So, tell me more about allergic rhinitis, hay fever, whatever it is. Are their chances that it might really turn into sinusitis?" Harrell asked.

"Do you know what Sinusitis is exactly? Dr. Connells asked.

"Cold and headache" Harrell answers.

"Not exactly," Connells said. "Sinusitis is inflammation of the sinuses, usually caused by bacterial or viral infection, or sometimes allergies. Facial pain and pressure, nasal congestion, thick mucus discharge, headache, and sometimes fever these are the symptoms."

"That is complicated, is it similar to Migraine?"

Dr. Connells said "No, they are all different. You know there are 3 conditions that are widely seen in today's generation which are causing pain and discomfort in everyday life. Sinusitis, migraine, and spondylitis are distinct medical conditions with different causes, symptoms, and treatments. Migraine is a neurological condition that can cause severe headaches and other symptoms. Spondylitis is an inflammation of the vertebrae, often associated with arthritis. I actually suffer from Spondylitis, due to intense study and research I have done, my neck posture was affected, I have to do a lot of exercise and sit in comfortable position, this is where it hurt the most". Connells turns and points at the spinal and back area where it is hurting.

Harrell asked, "Is your back pain unbearable? Is it also rare?"

"Where were you all this time? These three conditions are now becoming very common than common cold. Everywhere, you can find people suffering from at least one of these problems. Some people might have to go for surgeries." Dr Connells said sarcastically to Harrell

"Why does your name have an "s" it is Connells, not Connell?" Harrell asks to Dr. Connells Kimsons.

"When I was born, my father by mistake added "s" in my name, but he noticed the extra 's' when I started school. He said to keep it as it's similar to Kimsons's 's' "Connells says

"Why did you not change it to Connell?"

"I was habituated to it"

"Interesting"

Harrell said "If this problem has become very common then why there is no permanent solution for this disease."

Connells says "Because this medical condition is mostly managed by changing the life styles. Ironically, people have to focus on their health to keep going forward, it takes money to keep going forward. The question is do people should worry about their health or their basic needs like food, shelter and safety. It takes money to treat any health-related problem.

People have to work. The big companies, their management, want people to work harder, and governments keep introducing rules, eight hours used to be permanent working hour, now ten working hours are considered standard. Some will tell "why you need personal life if you want to successful professional life. You have to sacrifice to get success. So don't just live, work more and live less".

It is sad but it is going to get worse in future" Connells says to Harrell.

Harrell reply "Aren't those Management and government human too?"

Connells says "**This is how life is, we are all Social Animals**".

Chapter 7

Survival of the unfits.

"Social Animals, I understand what you mean."

As the sun began to set, the evening is starting to settle in the sky. The two strangers had now drifted into the philosophical conversation about the life of an animal, Humans. Why? For awareness.

"We live in pile; pretend we are better than wolves" Connells says.

"Better than wolfs, it is true though. We are better than them. To become an alpha, a leader, a wolf has to fight for real and other wolves that are defeated are controlled by fear to maintain stability in the pack. And we pretend to fight to live in a fake peace, where victories are decided by connections, not by strength. Poor are controlled and pushed. The rich get richer and more powerful. We are better, right?" Harrell sarcastically says to Connells and both started to laugh.

"We are all fighting to keep up with the pace of the world, even against diseases"

Harrell interrupt and says "Fight with diseases also."

"Yes, we are special right, so we have created Vaccines. Whenever a baby is born a number of vaccines need to be given. Whenever a viral disease starts spreading and threatens our existence. We create vaccines to make ourselves immune to those.

We are fighting with intelligence so that we could live more. One fact that remains undeniable, is human body is evolving or is it weakening?" Dr Connells says.

Harrell says "It is not about fight; it is not about peace either. It's about changing ourselves for better living. It's up to us, how we use our tools.

Either you fight against the flow of the wind or use the flow of wind to move to the places where you will be acknowledged, you will be crowned.

I know now that the life is not about love it is far more than that. I have a goal that is my bakery. I will definitely bring the change in my life, so that my peoples can live a better life. I am not saying we are living poorly. I just want us to have far more than what we have today.

To have more, you have to do more."

Harrell stood "Until our next meet Dr Connells, do drop by our bakery sometimes."

A little tilt, a little smile, the face looked down, watching the pair of brown sandal walking toward the door until the door slammed closed.

Connells sits there for two seconds after the footsteps. His eyes locked on the window until a lady in an orange dress passed by. Sipping his wine while he looks outside the window, he eventually saw nothing but the darkening street.

Harrell entered the bakery finding her mother and July chatting. She came to them; placed her sling bag on the table, put both hands on the table, and said, "World is very cruel place mom, we have to slowly sacrifice our comfort and heath to have better life. Everyone is suffering."

"Must be amazing date?" Veronica says to her daughter Harrell.

"Date? It was not a date, that Susanne told him about my...." Harrell said, but her mother interrupted her.

"I know, she came by in the afternoon, so what is Connells said."

"I don't have sinusitis, I have allergy" Harrell says walking back to her room.

"Hey! What? It was Allergy all this time.

Oh my!! Connells is really a good doctor" Veronica says to July while she sees her daughter going back to her room.

July says to Veronica "One thing is definitely different; may be it's the air."

Harrell wakes up to strange noise. One man is laughing. She starts to run toward the dining room, finding her brother Liam sitting with her mom, July, Maria and David, July's husband.

"Good morning RelRel" Liam.

"It's Harrell, how many times will I have to say this? What you are doing here?" Harrell says.

July said, "They have holidays so they have come for a few days to stay."

"Well, it is their house; they should be one who should live here." Harrell says back and sits one of empty table.

July seems to be a little hurt. Liam says sarcastically "A woman wakes up with her nose runny, puts her shots everywhere, to make her feel better."

"Mom, see he is again calling me snotty" Harrell complains.

"I am not saying about you, I am taking about a snotty woman. Are you a snotty woman?"

"Mom"

"Liam, leave her alone, now she found new man who taught her "World is cruel". And we come to know that she does not have sinusitis, it is kind of allergy" Veronica saying while gesturing Harrell to sit beside her.

"No Sinus problem, then what is it?" Liam says.

"Actually, it's my fault, Jade told me it is sinusitis and symptoms were also same at that time. Even when we went to doctor, instead of telling him about my symptoms, I let Jade do the all talking. And doctor also didn't argue. Even when I went to Dr. Kevin in Watsar, I told him I have sinusitis instead of explaining my whole situation.

Last week I went to Kimsons and Dr. Connells wanted to know all the details. He concluded that it is Hay fever something like cold rhinitis" Harrell Explains.

"So you taking medicines which was not supposed to take", Maria asks

"No, Dr. Kevin has asked me to take Anti-histamine only when my nose get watery, an allergic medicine as he though it is acute sinusitis. Rest all the medicines I had to take if my condition got worst. So, I took mostly anti-histamines. But when I was in Thown, I used to take the entire dose as doctor prescribed; maybe that's why I was drowsy all the time." Harrell clarifies.

"You are really dumb Relrel" Liam says

"Or may be Connell is great doctor" Veronica says

"It is Connells not Connell" Harrell says

Veronica replies "Sorry sorry, Its Dr. Connells Kimsons"

"Wow, Connells is still haven't changed his name." Liam says

"You know him" Harrell says

"Everyone here knows him, he is best doctor here and he has received awards for making some new medicines. His photo comes to newspaper many times" David says back.

"Really, he is that famous" Harrell says.

"Yep, he is a good guy, a little dull. Are you interested in him?" Liam asks.

"No, what is wrong with you, Mom why is he always like this" Harrell complain to her mom.

The room fills with laughter. After a long time, the laughter's are echoing in the Serene's house.

Harrell was sitting at the counter of the bakery in the afternoon. Liam walks in and stands beside Harrell looking outside the window. "Everything is going well in the bakery"

"Yes, what about you? Are your students bullying you?

"No, I have strict aura, they all fear me" Liam says.

"Really, you very scary, you are just mean. But I can't deny, people are scared of you. You know Vivi and Susanne they are still scared of you." Harrell says

"You know I have to be the Man of this house. I have to protect you and mom, since father was not here. I have to look at lots of things. You are very carefree; you do whatever you want and say whatever you feel" Liam replies.

"I am not so carefree, I am very mature" Harrell says.

"Really! Then why such coldness toward July and David, I am sensing that you don't like them from the moment you came back. I thought you will change but still you don't care what your words can hit." Liam asks.

"Well, if they want to stay with us, don't you think they should work with us. When I came, I saw Mom was the one working and July and David were just resting and eating."

"They didn't come here on their own; I requested David uncle to come live here so that I can go Watsar."

"Why can't you live here?" Harrell asks.

"Because I and Maria have jobs there in Watsar that pays us a good handsome salary, which this bakery can't bake." Liam answer.

"It takes 1 hour by bus to go Watsar, can't you and your wife can travel…" Harrell got angry

"Listen, Harrell you know me from the beginning, I didn't learn how to bake bread. I learned to teach so that I can have Job.

I know this Bakery cannot support all of us after Father left.

Do you think that I want to leave the place where I was born willingly?

And I know one thing for sure; you can never accept other people's kindness. I know you don't like Maria either. Neither July and David nor Diana and Ron. But you need to keep in mind that they were with Mom when you left this house to marry that City king Jade."

Liam stops when he sees a Man Waiting in the Door.

"Hello" Connells enters the Bakery at event of sibling fighting.

"Hey Man, can you keep the door open, I need to... Aww... Connells Sir, you are here? Welcome" David comes with empty bags inside the Bakery.

"Thank you, nice to meet you." Connells hold the Door for David

"Oh! You must have been tired, thank you David, Here sit" Harrell take the 2 big bags from David and bring him a glass of Water. "How was today, did all the deliveries went well?"

David answers "Yep, today everything went well, and here are the orders for tomorrow, The Clover Bakery said they need extra muffins and three baked cakes as there are some Birthday Party orders."

"Great, you can rest or shall I bring something to eat here." Harrell asks

"No No, here is the bag and I put the bill here itself; I will go inside. I bought some hair clips for July. I will go and give her, otherwise I will forget."David gives the bag to Harrell before he went inside the house.

"What Deliveries?" Liam asks.

David answers "Oh Liam you don't know right, we have started delivery services as per order basis from last 3 months so that we can sell more. We sell our bread to other Bakeries in the neighbouring towns. Harrell says we have to expand our market to expand our profits. Sorry, Harrell told me not to tell you about these things."

“But why we need to deliver?” Liam asks

Harrell sat and started counting the Money and look at Liam from the corner of her eye. “You know this “Bakery cannot support all of us since father left” so we need to find way to sell more breads, simply increasing customer”

Liam’s face twisted in shock, as if he had smelled something unpleasant.

“By the way, Can I have one banana bread and half a loaf of wheat bread please” Connells says.

“Oh! Dr. Connells, I forgot about you, actually Banana Bread is sold out, here try some muffins they are great!!” Harrell put a Muffin on plate and places on table. Move a chair and gesture Connells to sit “Come sit here”.

Liam sees Connells as of lasers were shooting from his eyes. And then he goes back to kitchen with heavy bouncy walks

“Wrong timing” Connells says.

“It’s nothing, my brother is very overprotective and he hates change” Harrell sits in front of Connells.

“What is changing? Connells asked.

“Actually, when I went to city, I saw few bakeries just sell but not making them originally. So I though what if we sold to that kind of Bakery with our Name “The Serene Bakery”, then people will see our Name in this packet and then they will come back to us, and say, Are you the “The Serene Bakery”, can we have your breads? We heard your bread is very tasty." Harrell explain by showing the packaging she has designed.

"Nice Plan! So, your brother is worried about you, am I right? Connells ask while eating the muffins.

"Is it tasty?" Harrell asks

Connells replies "Yes, very very tasty"

Behind the Bakery, Liam goes to Kitchen finding his mom and July making some preparation and Maria sitting on the chair, arranging some berries in different boxes.

"Mom, why didn't you tell me? Harrell is making huge changes here." Liam complains

Maria stands and walks in the Kitchen. Veronica looks at his worried son and July say "Here we go! I told you he will react like this if he knows that we are building a small factory"

"Factory?" Liam screams

"Relax; it's not a Factory, just a small unit with Baking Machines for mass production." Veronica led her son outside by the backdoor through the dining table by putting her hand on this back. Maria & July follows them.

There was new room built in the backyard, you could still smell the fresh cement in the air. Veronica opened the door to an empty room with granite slabs attached to the walls, two sinks with water lines. She turned on the light, "See this is not big, just 2 rooms connect with an arch, she going to install 2 big ovens here and here is the machine to mix the flour will come. You can see this place; here the packing of the bread will be done by hands. Harrell has visited many bakeries in Watsar, Dogel, and Thown and even she went to capital Bilbird with David. She met many people and asked for good advices. Also, we are buying machine not from shop but from guy name Conil in Dogel, he makes those machines and sells. We got good discounts as he is cousin of Louise Parker, Vivi's husband."

"But still you should have told me" Liam says.

"I told them not to..." Maria interrupts.

"What? You know about them." Liam asks

"Yes, Harrell did tell me and even asked for my advice and I think that is best for her. Instead of focusing on her failed marriage, it is better for her to focus on this.

I do understand whether the bakery in this village will work out or not. But if you try to understand what Harrell is trying to do here, you will definitely decide to support her." Maria assures.

"It is not like I will not support her. I am her brother. I care for her but do you think this is okay, if she wants to put real money in a decision like this just to distract herself from the loser Jade and her failed marriage. I don't think this is right?" Liam says.

"See this is what I was concerned about you. You cannot accept anything new. You don't trust things easily. You need to understand this is not just a makeover for her. She wants to do something which is valuable and will be for good and better living for this family. Everyone has opposed her at first. But she has convinced everyone, even me." Maria says back to Liam with the confidence of a Lady Empress.

"You know Liam; I thought she was naive at first but she is not. She is smart with hot pepper tongue" July interrupts them.

"You know what she always said to me "the only thing we have to fear is fear itself". I don't even know what she means. She is scared but still doesn't want to give up. And we also think this is good for all of us. You have no idea; we are getting order on every 2-3 days. Even when Harrell, David, Diana and Ron come to help us, we still have to overwork to finish these orders. We really need these machines now".

Liam lean back toward the wall and four people are standing in silence. Yes, the changes are annoying some people crave them and some try to resist. It cannot be ignored.

And you know what is wonderful or dreadful about changes, the small the change take more time than the bigger the changes.

Small changes take a massive amount of time. Massive changes come in the blink of an eye. The world turns around, which will make us feels agony, weird and anger.

"When will it be installed" Liam asks.

"In next 2 weeks" Veronica confirms.

Liam starts to walk back to the house, but stop at the door. "Do I look this stubborn to you?"

"No, we wanted to include you in this decision, but Harrell want to show and wanted to surprise you. You know she looks up to you most. She wants to be acknowledged by you" Veronica says to her elder son. Looking at his back, she knows he is happy.

Here in the bakery Madam Harrell is talking non-stop to Connells about her future plan. And Connells is trying to go out but his foot is currently nailed to the ground. The nail was made of Harrell voice.

Connells stops Harrell, "Do you think this will work out?"

"It is working out fine; I have not taken any liability from anyone, I making this on the basis of revenue we are making from last four month. I am not that smart but I am very keen. My small steps are spontaneous. The moment you get the opportunity; you have to grab it." Harrell says.

"Have you ever heard about the Turtle and Rabbit story" Connells asked to Harrell.

"Slow and steady wins the race, that why Turtle won" Liam disrupted the flow of air in the room with sudden bark. "But the problem here is our Harrell here is not Rabbit that will sleep in the middle of the forest. You know why?"

"Why?" Connells mumbled.

"Because our Relrel have allergies. When she will try to sleep in middle of forest, she will get all snotty and start to sneeze, then to find her medicine and tissues, she will run like crazy and end up winning the race" Liam say by putting his hand on Harrell.

"How can you say that about your sister?" Harrell started pouting. Liam bent his knee so his eyes could be in same line with Harrell, "When my sister becomes the eldest in this house. Still, I do not support your decision, but I will support you."

Harrell became pink like lilies.

"You know father always used to say to me "Your only strength is you but never underestimate your people walking beside you" Liam adds and look at Connells.

"So, this is your new Boyfriend, Nelnels meet Relrel" Liam put his hand toward Connells for handshake.

"What are you saying?" Harrell burst. "Nice to meet you Connells, still with extra "S". Planning to remove it or not" Liam says to Connells

"No, he is habituated to it." Harrell screams.

The two men look at each other then look at the confident Harrell with a tilted face.

"Well heard about you and Paula, Sorry about that."

"No worries, I have long forgotten about it. Okay then I take my leave, thank you Harrell, See you again Liam. Bye" Leaving the sibling behind in the bakery.

"Paula, who is she?" Harrell asked.

"Paula is the eldest daughter of Mr Gabriel". Liam confirms.

"The one who got married last month" Harrell asks. Liam answers "yes, she used to be in relationship with Connells. They dated for more than 5 years but when she went to Watsar to live in with him. Suddenly we got the news that she has been engaged to Connells best friend George Natwon, a general surgeon. And then she got married to him. Connells didn't even come to their wedding. That was rough time for him. His father also died, his friend betrayed and had a breakup due to cheating.

World is cruel, right? When it gives, it gives very little; when it takes, it takes everything."

"I didn't know that, but Connells is such great man, I don't understand why she left him"

"Well, the other guy was General surgeon; you know how much they earn. And Connells is a son of Kimsons so obviously she will choose him over Connells. Everyone is competing to have better life. Even you are trying your best to level up.

Not everyone chooses the right pathways. Some people try too hard to get better and better, by using other as a ladder to go up, they don't even bother if others might get hurt in the middle. Such people are like Snakes.

You know the game Snakes and Ladder; it is actually reality. Some are snake and some are ladder. Some put you up and some poison you to throw you down. Every step should be taken very carefully in life, who knows, some might be like a ladder that will help us to go up but the real snakes are always waiting for opportunity to push you down.

This world will never be fair."

Harrell says "it's like we are living in the Jungle, Survival of the Fittest.

But you know everyone is suffering either mentally and physically.

The new term is **Survival of the Unfits.**"

Chapter 8

Being human is hard.

As summer was coming to an end, the land became thirsty. The rain gathered in the sky, ready to say "hi" to its old friends, and June has begun. Harrell became good friends with Connells; they used to meet either in Serene Bakeries when Connells comes for shopping or in the Kimsons either for treatment or friendly hangout along with Susanne, and Vivi.

In their Mini truck, Harrell and Uncle David were driving back to their village, Pallena, after making a delivery of cupcakes and rum cakes for a party in Watsar. "I am really tired," Harrell confessed. "Do you think we can keep doing this?

David said "Well it is the start, but we need to keep going like this. The more order we get, the more beneficial it is for our business."

"Yes, it is… here here, Liam asked us to stop here" Harrell asked David for a sudden stop near the Bus stop at the outskirt of Watsar. A guy in brown pants and a white shirt appeared with a lady in a formal grey gown. It was Liam and his wife Maria.

"You guys took a lot of time; I have been waiting for you from last one hour," Liam says.

"It was just a wait of only 15 minutes dear." Maria says while sitting inside the Mini truck beside Harrell. "No worries, we all know him. Are you able to sit, here move this side." Harrell says while they adjust in the small sit in the front.

"Okay then, we will go." David says

"Fine, take care Maria; I will come home this weekend." Liam says.

"Sure, will you be alive alone Liam" Harrell says

"Have a safe drive, bye bye" Liam says

The mini-truck start again to his way to Pallena as words left out from the window, "Don't ignore me…!"

"What happened, Maria? Suddenly you want to come to Pallena for rest, is something very serious. My mother said you are not feeling well with all the city noise and stuff. I think I know, you wanted a break, right? He is very dominant." Harrell says.

Maria says "Well, part of reason is your brother stubbornness, but I wanted to take long break from work. And with all the noise I couldn't stay there. Even Liam's high-toned voice was hurting my head."

"What seriously, I thought you were just a little bit sick." Harrell says

"Kid, you didn't get it right" David says. Harrell reply "What? Did I miss something?"

"I am pregnant dear. We found out last week. Liam was getting very protective of me, you don't to go to work, take leaves, but then I have to go to work, because we need more money, but then who will take care of you, no wait, let me ask Mom to come, but then who will work in bakery, You and David travel most of the time.

Don't sit here, don't move too much. Tell me what you need. A simple noise and he will come running to me, what happen, what happen, are you ok? Are you hurt?

So, I thought it would be better if I stayed with you guys. In Watsar, the air is polluted because of the factories. And I thought Pallena would be a great place to stay. Even Liam will be rest assured that I have people around me who can take care of me.

Even after marriage, I never stayed in Pallena more than 4-5 days.

I thought it would be a good opportunity. I want to know more about Pallena, Liam's place" Maria says as the cold breeze enters the congested but comforting miniature truck of them.

The Sun was setting down; the cloud becomes yellow, pink and purple. And finally, the board came "3km - Pallena" on the side of road. Here comes the village of Harrell & Connells, Pallena.

As you enter the village, you can see sky bursts with warm hues of orange and purple, bathing the homes in a soft, ethereal glow. Smokes are curling from a few chimneys from home, and the scent of wood smoke mingles with the earthy smell of the fields as the day winds down, the village people have started preparing for dinner and for the nights. The peaceful scene is amplified by the silhouette of trees against the vibrant sky and the quiet sounds of evening settling over the landscape.

"Isn't it so peaceful, I knew when I come here, I will feel refresh" Maria words flew, increasing the ambience of the village.

"Mom, we are back" Harrell entered the house from side door.

"Where Maria, oh my child, I heard the good news, finally a new flower will bloom in our Serene house." Veronica came out and gave a warm hug to her daughter-in-law Maria.

"How was the business dear?" July comes out, and took the bag from David and walked with him in the house, followed by Harrell.

The yellow light glowed in the dining hall, all five were sitting at the table with cups of tea and chatting about the days, while the dinner was slowly cooking in the kitchen.

A sudden knock on the door, a girl named Joana comes and asks for Ron. "Hi! Joana how's school?" Harrell asks Joana after calling Ron. Joana replies "Yes, everything is going fine; the new syllabus is looking very tough?"

"Oh really! Then it will take two people to finish the whole homework, right?" Harrell jokes.

"Thank you, Harrell, now you can go back" Ron comes, signalling Harrell to go back into the house.

"By god, just look at him, he is really becoming like Liam." Harrell goes back to the room. "Love is blooming everywhere." A voice comes from outside, Suzanne enters the house while she crosses the teen couple.

"Hey, Harrell, what are you doing?" Susanne enters. "Nothing just having tea, what happened? Is it something urgent?" Harrell says while pouring another cup of tea and giving to Susanne.

Can we talk in your room? Susanne asks.

"Sure dear" Veronica says while everyone smiles.

In the Harrell room, Susanne enters putting her bag on the table, "I am going to use your washroom real quick." as she says she goes to the washroom to get freshen up. She came back from her office directly to Harrell house. While Harrell sat, a small moment recapped in her head, where she has been noticing that Susanne was behaving a little strangely for a few weeks; she does not want to go outside but always want to hangout either at her place or Vivi's house. And even when Harrell asks her out, she refuses saying she doesn't want to eat outside. Susanne had been started behaving strange from last month. Harrell decided that this time she will surely going to dig the secret out.

"Sorry dear, I just came from office and needed to talk to you so I thought it would be best to barge in to your house." Susanne comes back to the room and sits on a cushioned chair, took the cup from the table and started to drink.

"Is it cold?"

"No, it's still warm"

"So, what is it? You wanted to share something with me?" Harrell asked, leaning forward.

"Share? Nothing just wanted to ask you something." Susanne says

"Hmm… go on…. I am listening" Harrell speak with interval of drinking her leftover tea.

"Will you be my bridesmaid?" Susanne asks.

"Huh!! You going to get married, who is the guy? When? Wait why suddenly?"

"I got pregnant so, now I am getting married?"

"Hmm... Pregnant… Really?"

"Yep"

"Who is the father? And… who will the groom?"

"Victor is the father, and he is the groom, what you think of me?" Susanne says casually.

"When is the wedding?"

"Next week, on the 12th of June"

Harrell stands up. "In eight days, you are getting married, and you are telling me now."

"What in 8 days you are getting married? And I am hearing like this" Vivi says with a plate of cookies in her hand.

"Why you are here?" Susanne asks Vivi, to which Vivi reply while eating cookies like popcorn, "I saw you entering Harrell house, so I asked Louise to look after the kids and ran here."

A moment of silence for the ladies, please. The three friends gathered for an unexpectedly serious talk, but each occupied a different emotional space: the bride-to-be sipped her tea with no worries, the visibly pregnant friend contentedly finishing her cookies, and the third staring at the ceiling, her messy hair framing a mouth agape as her eyes meticulously calculate the whole situation.

"How did this happen?" Harrell asks.

"That not how you ask. When did you find out that you are pregnant and how Victor proposed you." Vivi asked.

"It is a bit complicated, I find out about my pregnancy on May 17th, 2 weeks ago. And I told Victor. He said he wanted me to have an abortion. I refused. Then he said, "I don't want this child" and walked out. So, I found out about his father and mother and went to his parents' house. Then I told them everything about it and asked them to convince Victor to think about marriage as I want to keep this child and I like Victor too. We both have almost the same job. And I have a good income. His Mother and Father said if they didn't agree what would I do?

I said, I will be going to have this child. If he does not agree, I will try to find someone who might get married to me. If there is no other option left then I will file a complaint against Victor to take responsibility. But I would give birth to this child.

But when Victor came to his house and saw me. He got irritated and was about to push me. So, his father stopped him and slapped him. His father said, "You are not a Man, I am ashamed that I am your father." And his mother reconfirmed if I was right and wrong.

At first, he said I am lying but then his mother also slaps him, "Do you think we do not know about this, everyone in Pallena know that you guys are dating."

But Victor said, "He will never be going to marry a girl like me and left the house".

His father and mother consoled me and said not to worry, they will be going to convince Victor so please don't file any complaints against him for now. I said, "I will wait for one week and left the house".

Then after four days, Victor, Mr. Tucker and Mrs. Tucker came to my house. And I had a serious discussion with my grandma. They liked my house very well. At last, I told my grandma that I can handle Victor, I want him to be my husband, Grandma also agreed.

Then after some time the wedding date was set as June 12th. Victor is still mad at me, but he talks very nicely with me. He is not happy though" Susanne tells her friend about the whole event led to her wedding.

"What, you are forcing Victor to get married to you, what if he does something to you after marriage?" Harrell says with concern.

"Good job dear, this is how you should treat these men; they want all the pleasure but refuse to take responsibility." Vivi says while patting Susanne's back.

"What? Why praise her? Susanne you cannot force someone to marry you, what if he hurts you and behaved violently toward you?" Harrell asks with concern.

"I knew you will react like this that is why I wanted to talk to you alone. But listen I know Victor very well, I like him and he also liked me until I was pregnant, things will work out fine in future. He is right now upset, because he is feeling like his freedom is going away. But I think he will be fine when he sees our child." Susanne says coldly.

"Dear, listen I don't care about anyone else here except for you." Harrell holds the hand of Susanne and looks in her eyes with worry, concern and pain.

"Why you are sympathizing with her, when you should stand with her in confidence. You should motivate her" Vivi stops Harrell.

"This is not right" Harrell quarrels

"This is not wrong either." Vivi quarrels back.

"Why this is not wrong here?" Harrell asks.

"Because Susanne pregnant, she has his baby. He is the father. Can't you see Victor is trying to run away until she tells his family about the consequences and look for the first time, Susanne is taking responsibility here? Also, she wants Victor to get serious to take responsibility. And in the end, he agreed. What is wrong here?" Vivi says to Harrell.

"Can't you see Victor agreed because he is afraid that Susanne might file a complaint? That is why he agreed. How can I let my best friend get married to someone who is such a bad person? I didn't like Victor from the beginning. I knew he was playing with you." Harrell says

"Well, fairly speaking, we both were playing with each other." Susanne smiles

"You are smiling, I don't understand, why?"

Vivi sits on the bed, "Harrell do you know how I got married?"

"Weren't you and Louise were in love, and you got pregnant" Harrell answers.

"No, Louise was interested in you at first, but you were never bothered to talk to him. I liked him, but he never looked at me. One day he approached me in the classroom for some stupid notes and used to meet me occasionally afterward. I knew he was using me to get close to you. Instead of helping him to get close to you, I purposely told him to tell his true feeling to you. I know all along you will reject him. When you rejected him, he was hurt. After sometime I asked him out. We started dating and I eventually became pregnant. He was worried at first, but he was one who proposed to me for marriage. He never shown any interest in you from the moment we came in relationship. We have 2 sons and now the 3rd one is on the way. Do you know why me, and Louise is happy… well not happy but peacefully married for the last 6 years? Vivi asked Harrell.

"Because Louise is responsible person and he cares for you, you do the same, you are made of each other" Harrell says.

Vivi says "There are no soul mates because no one is made for another; we build our connections by working things out. Successful relationships are the result of people working together. Louise is a gentleman, but he also gets angry & frustrated too. But we know how to make things comfortable for each other.

We are each other's safety net and punching bags too. That is what marriage is for me.

How can we truly assess a person's character from afar, when it often takes living with someone for five to ten years to truly know if they are good or bad?

A marriage lasts by working on it every day to make it last until the next day.

Sorry to say but weren't you and Jade in love. Then a small disease made him change his attitude toward you. You felt lonely and like a burden. You left Jade not because you want him to be free to live his dream but because you wanted to free yourself for being a burden. Am I wrong here?"

Harrell was silent; she couldn't agree but she also couldn't disagree.

Is it wrong to force someone to take responsibility for their actions, or can a person maintain a positive attitude that a happy family will eventually form, despite being built on coercion? Think about it. When a woman wants to have a child and also wants the father to be involved, but he is unwilling, she might use the law to enforce his responsibilities; this raises the question of whether it is ethical to force parenthood, or if she should consider abortion, asking another man to step in, or raising the child alone.

A woman wants the child, but she wants the father to be there for the child. If he does not listen, she uses the law and its power to control him. Let's say Susanne is wrong here, then should she abort the child or go and beg another man to take responsibility, or even greater option, be righteous, raise the child on her own without father's name.

Society is a group of different kinds of people. Each one has its own role. If a person empowers, he or she will be going to dominate others who are weaker. Not only that he or she will use the power to ensure their future generation can live better lives.

Powerful people seize and maintain their positions, fighting for their "kingdoms" just like lions; if "survival of the fittest" is the rule of the world, why then is it considered wrong for them to use that power to benefit themselves and their descendants?

The principle of "survival of the fittest" demonstrates that the world is, by its very nature, unfair.

The most advanced creature on earth, the human being, has survived countless disasters and diseases by constantly adapting and inventing, but this very drive to innovate stems from a paradoxical state of never being satisfied, a trait that is both their greatest flaw and most powerful advantage.

Because humans constantly try to benefit themselves, some great legend stood on the frontline and created an amazing system, the "System of Law". The Law regulate a society, human behaviours and their actions for maintaining order, resolving the disputes, making sure justice prevails. Laws, rules and codes of conduct promote fairness and social well-being. While people may propose changing the law, possibly for their own or their group's benefit, the necessity or justification for such alterations cannot always be clearly defined

As long as a rope can be used to ensure a horse travels in a controlled direction and its rider remains safe, one might be tempted to say, "Wow, humans can control a horse." But if that rope is too tight, it will hurt the animal. The simple presence of a rope used to tie a living creature presents a clear moral conflict: one can justify its use for the sake of order and safety, preventing a dangerous situation, but this same action denies the being its freedom, forcing it into a controlled, rather than a wild, existence.

That is how law enforcement works by restricting a human being's desire to be completely wild and free, law defines paths that maintain social order and peace, ultimately helping to end conflict.

Vivi says "Harrell, listen, nothing ever goes as planned in this world. The longer we live, the cruel it will become, and we must sometimes take decisions that might crumble our principles. Reality is painful & suffering might come. But we have to keep moving forward.

What did Susanne do, right or wrong, is different here? Think about the child. Do you want this child not to stay with his own father, not to have his father's name? Do you have any how society will treat this child? And it's Victor's child so one day he going to accept him entirely."

Harrell look at Vivi and then look at Susanne and ask, "How are holding up?"

"Scared to death?" Susanne replied.

Harrell takes the hand of Susanne, gives her a gentle hug and softly brushes her back, "I will stand beside you as your bridesmaid."

"Okay guys I need to go rest; I will leave, have a lot to do." Susanne says while taking her stuff. She put a hand on Harrell's shoulder, "I don't have Papa and Mama. But I have you, Vivi and Grandma.". With these words, Susanne walks out of the Room.

"Bye dear," Vivi says, "I am sorry if you got hurt by my words."

"No, I am not, am thankful for your words. I thought you are just a dumb girl, I never thought you can be intelligent too" Harrell says while she stays inside the room. Vivi leaves the room with an angry face, mumbling something like "Ha I am dumb, I look dumb, what is wrong with my face, these people.... ah whatever.... Huh...."

Diana comes to room, "Harrell lets go Dinner is ready."

"Hmm. Coming"

"What happened? Is everything okay?" Diana asks by looking at her sister.

"Nothing is wrong," Harrell says "It's just that **being human is hard**.

Chapter 9

Behave Maturely!!

In the middle of the night, a man enjoying his loneliness with a glass of scotch. The dimly lit room was disturbed by sudden thunder.

"Rain has come finally. Again, there's going to be mud everywhere. No dry land, only wet mud. Ahh… When is this government going to build roads in this village? I live with no roads." Connells drunken talk echoes through the room.

Suddenly the door opens; a figure with a big pointy cap appears.

"A witch, why are you here?" Connells says.

A Manly voice came "I am not a witch."

"Hmm… wizard?"

"Not a wizard either, how many glasses have you had?" Victor Tucker sits beside Connells after taking out his weird pointy cap.

"What happened, I thought you would be with your dear girlfriend" Connells asks with the sleepy voice.

"Dear girlfriend, my foot, she is forcing me to get married to her now." Victor says after pouring a glass of the same bottle Connells was drinking.

"Why did you get her pregnant?" Connells words bring a sudden pause in the moment. "Congratulations, at least you are not dying alone" Connells say to Victor.

Victor after taking a sip of the scotch, "Do you know what she said to me, if I don't marry her now, she files a complaint against me.

"Why did she do that?"

"Yes, I knew that you would understand me, my mom and father are praising her and want me to be married soon. They said that a girl would come to us instead of going to the police because she has some kind of hope that we will accept her. She seems nice and is a civil worker. And I am aloof. Shouldn't parents protect their child instead of listening to another girl." Victor Complains.

Connells say, "That is what is being said: why did she do that?" Isn't this your job to protect your own child? You are the father here. You should accept the child on your own. The question is, why has she taken such critical steps, using the law to make it clear that you are the father? Are you Man or not? Don't make us judge you? Do what a real Man does in this situation."

"What about my life? Don't I have the right to choose my life partner?" Victor asks.

"Where were those thoughts when you were being romantic?" Connells say sarcastically.

Victor burst "You don't get it. It's been 1 year since I started my job in my post office, and I was welcomed by Susanne in the post office. Before we could even decide, we started dating and then suddenly she comes and told me "Let's get married, because I am pregnant." My whole life has collapsed now."

Connells tries to make Victor understand, "You know Victor; I have my whole life planned. Had a girlfriend from college day, she moved in with me and she used to talk to me about our future and all. But one day she comes to me and confesses that she does not like me anymore. She wants a breakup.

I was taken back but I realise the distance between us from the moment she moved in. I thought maybe I am wrong, I cannot make her happy, and I couldn't make her stay. But after 1 week, I found her with my best friend George; we were friends from college. She was sitting with him like they were in love from eternity. Then I realized it was not me who couldn't make her stay. It was her, who never wanted to stay. It is fortunate to have a tsundere girl who is beautiful, talkative, and responsible."

Victor says with an unnoticed smile "Tsundere, yep she is kind of one".

"So did you agree?" Connells asks

"Yep, even if she behaves like this, she is Susanne." Victor stands up and takes his hat. "Come to church hall on 12 June around morning 6 AM."

Connells says "That is too early for me, can't I come at late."

"No, you have come early, you are my best man, and you will have a lot of jobs to do on that day. Bye" Victor says and leaves.

"Do I have any right to my life? Why do people come and go on their own and tell what to do? As if I will go? Never" Connells says with heavy eyes.

12th June, the Wedding Day, a beautiful morning with birds chirping and flying a cool, light breeze moving under the clear sky. Sun has just rise making the sky shine with golden light. A Man wearing brown coat appears in front of the Church, which is yet to open, with a small box rapped in red gift paper. When he looked around no was found. He looked at his watch, the time was correct, it was 6 AM in the morning.

"Where is everyone?" Connells asked.

"Hey, are you Connells Kimsons?" A man asks through the window of mini truck with flower and tents in the back.

"Yes, we need to make arrangement here for the wedding of "Tucker - Stone". Is this the correct location?"

Connells say "Yes, this is where the wedding is going to happen?"

Sunlight can create a beautiful design in the church with white and pink flowers placed in a few places. The decoration was simple, but elegant. The awe-inspiring atmosphere says today is a special day. Something is going to change for sure. A woman sitting in her old designed wedding dress of her grandma, which is altered making it more elegance and radiance. The radiating a sense of joy and anticipation can be seen on her face.

"You are looking beautiful", Veronica says to the nervous bride Susanne.

Everyone was busy; suddenly Susanne heard a voice from the window. She leans and asks who. The answer comes, "It's me". She knew right away it was her Groom.

"Go away! Don't you know it's bad luck for the bride and groom to see each other before the wedding? Susanne whispered through the window.

"No, you need to listen this before our wedding"

"What?"

"I want to apologize for my behaviour over the past few days, I really like… love you. I was very shocked when I found out that you were pregnant. I am sorry I tried to run away. But I will not run away anymore. I will assure you that I will protect you and our baby with all my strength. I cannot change past. But I will rewrite our future. So don't worry, just enjoy today as this is the day of our celebration. This wedding is a celebration of two mature fools." Victor says with all his might. Susanne smiles and replies "I knew Victor; I knew you will never run away. Thank you for saying those words".

As Victor smiles, suddenly his eyes meet with other guys who were standing on the other side of the other window. "Hello, Mr. Tucker, May I have a word with you?"

"Sure, but who are you?" Victor asks.

"Jade Stone, Susanne's Brother" Jade says while gesturing him to stay there, "I will there in a minute, please stay there".

"Sure, Mr Stone" Victor knew he messed up real good.

The backside of the church was a neglected garden with dry land, where the sacred met the untamed, lending a quiet, rustic charm. Victor was looking down and regretting being not careful with words as Jade come in the backyard along with a man who seems much older and far scarier.

Before they could speak, they were interrupted by two Man & one Women walking in the backyard from different directions.

"We are looking for you Mr. Groom" Harrell spoke as soon as she saw Victor.

"Why are you here, the ceremony is about to start, are you planning to run away now?" Harrell asks furiously.

"No, never, I was just going to come. Just a moment I need to talk to Mr. Stone. Give me a moment please. Hello Sir, nice to meet you! I am Victor Tucker" Victor said as he put his hand forward to Jade.

While they are shaking hands, Connells asks "Who is this Handsome man, I never seen them in village?"

"He is Son of a B**ch," Liam whispered angrily. "Oh, so that's Harrell's husband, a very successful lawyer, but no one ever mentioned how good-looking he is" Connells whispers as his eyes meet with angry Liam. "Ahn... You know there is a special kind of flower being used for decoration. Want to come with me to see those flowers" Liam reacted with a startled "Huh!" but before he could say anything more, Connells was already started walking fast. "I will go then," Connells said as he headed for the exit.

"Hello Jade, how are you?" Harrell asks.

"He seems fine, can't you see?" Liam says.

"I am fine Harrell, how are you?" Jade replies.

Liam interrupts again, "She is also fine."

"Harrell, it always nice to meet you" a man said, opening his arms. He had a white beard. It was Brian Stones, father of Jade and ex-father-in-law of Harrell.

Harrell returned with a warm hug, "How have you been? I came to known from Susanne that you have become an entrepreneur. Your Serene Bakery is getting famous around."

"Yes, things are working out very well. How are you? How's your health? How's Carol?" Brain asked.

"Well, everything is working out fine, but with your absence it took some time for us to adjust" Brian says. "And how is Liam, you have taken an oath to look charming every day or what?"

"Well, Sir I do try to." Liam answers.

Harrell smiles and says "I need to go see the preparation. Victor, we are waiting for in the hall." As she left followed by Liam, but Liam had no mercy look in his eyes for Jade.

"You know each other" Victor asks.

"Yes, she is my daughter like, Susanne's childhood friend. And we heard the things you have been doing for the last few days. Behaving badly? Running away?" Brian asked as he put out his cigar.

Jade says while looking directly to Victor, "It was our job to come early and settle everything for my dear sister. We are very sorry, we were late. You didn't think that Susanne is all alone, right?"

"No, she did mention about you guys." Victor says.

"Don't be afraid, dear; today is your wedding day, as it is for my daughter, Susanne," Brian said, exhaling smoke into the air. "It is going to be late, so why don't you go to the hall. But before you walk out, know this very clearly: the Stone family is famous for our law firm, one of the most successful in this country. Susanne is half-owner of this company. Just because her real father and mother died doesn't mean she is an orphan. We always had an eye on her, and now we will have one on you, too. One simple mistake can ruin anyone's life, and your poor judgment can do the same for you. Have a nice wedding day!"

Harrell walked to the bride's waiting room to tell Susanne it was time to go; but as Susanne, Vivi, and Veronica began walking toward the hall, Harrell, carrying the emergency bridal kit, was interrupted by a well-dressed woman, Carol Stone.

"Hello Harrell. Nice to see you again." Carol said.

Harrell replies "Long time no see, Carol. I sorry, I am little busy, I need to go..."

Before you go, I would like to express some gratitude, Harrell, I want to say thank you." Carol says.

"Thank you? Why suddenly? You were so happy when we got divorced." Harrell asks

"Oh, I'll be honest," Carol chirped, in a voice dripping with saccharine false sincerity "Well, it's true I don't like you," she said slowly, as if explaining a complex theory. "But it doesn't mean you're a bad person. No, no. You taught us a valuable lesson, "True bravery lies in acknowledging and accepting your flaws openly, even if it casts you as the villain in the eyes of others".

Thank you being a Villain in our lives."

Harrell's face remained as blank as a tombstone. "The pleasure was all mine," she replied with a dry, flat finality, and walked away with a serene, unnerving pride.

Finally, the wedding ceremony started. Susanne walks to the altar with her father's elder brother, Brian Stone. Both the groom and bride say their vows and finally become husband and wife. The small but lively wedding was attended by only a few close people. The wedding cake was cut, toast was made, a few danced and in the afternoon the couple made their departure. Harrell finished packing some stuff in the bride's room and leaving the place. A man approached her. It was her ex-husband, Jade.

"Can I speak with you for moment?" Jade asks politely.

"Sure, how are you, is everything going fine with work? Anything new?" Harrell asks.

"Yes somehow, I joined Dad's company after you left and I want to tell you that I am getting married around this year," Jade informs.

"Good to know Jade, I'm glad." Harrell congratulates him.

"How's your health, you are looking fine now, is sinusitis better?"

"Actually, I don't have Sinusitis. I have allergy, Allergy rhinitis."

"What, it's not sinusitis.... it's good to hear, so the treatment is going well?"

"I don't need treatment now; I just have to take a few precautions and some changes around."

"Great!!"

"I remember, you used to have headaches, right? Why don't you talk to my doctor? He is very famous; he has even received National awards, Dr Connells Kimsons, the best man; you met him today, right?" Harrell said with good intention.

"You know, Harrell, I wanted to confess something," Jade said. "I've hidden a few things from you. Before our wedding, and even before we started dating, I had a girlfriend named Sara. We were in love and wanted to get married, but her father opposed it, which led to our breakup. I was very depressed, but then I met you, and you changed things around.

"Why didn't her father let you both marry?" Harrell asks.

"It's because of my migraines," Jade confesses, and Harrell, taken aback, asks, "Migraines? You never told me." At that moment, Connells interrupts, walking beside Harrell. "Is that why you were so particular that Harrell has sinusitis? Correct me if I am wrong," he says, glaring angrily at Jade. Enraged, Jade snaps, "I am speaking with my ex-wife; could you do us a favour and leave?"

"He will not leave. We will leave together," Harrell tells Jade. "Just a last message: thank you for freeing me from the guilt of divorcing you. I hope you can become more honest with your next partner, so that she is able to win your trust for real."

Harrell left the church; her eyes filled with rage and distrust.

"You don't have to be so shocked, Mr. Jade," Connells said, following after her. "You're the one who made her like this, and now it's hard for her to trust any other man."

Jade suddenly heard a giggle. His eyes met with Liam and Maria, who were standing against the wall.

"Serves you right," Liam commented sarcastically.

Maria sighed, "Liam... **behave maturely**."

Chapter 10

Isn't it the Peace, that everyone chooses in the end?

The man was walking beside the frustrated woman. He knew that saying even a single word right now would be nothing less than inviting himself into a dangerous situation. The most dangerous creature in this world is a man who has nothing to loss and a silent woman who is not showing any emotion.

Harrell was walking back to her house and Connells was following two steps behind her.

"Harrell, where are you going?"

"I am going home?"

"But we are going in the other direction; your house is in the opposite direction."

Harrell stopped and looks around. They are now on the outskirts of their village, beside a beautiful farm of wheat fields. She found a big rock and sits on it. Connells wait; he sees the sky is still blue; Sunset is near but has not set yet. He looked at his watch; it was around 4. He walks towards Harrell and sits beside her on the ground.

"I don't know you very well. But I have known you for the last 2-3 months. From that experience I can say one thing clearly that you are not upset with your ex-husband confession. But why do you look so disappointed?" Connells asked.

Harrell replies "Why people get married? Is Love not enough?" Harrell asks. "Why was Victor being happy marrying Susanne even when she threatens him? I know that marriage is about working along to become a family every day. But then why do people look for love first then after that they think "Should they married or not?"

Love is not the reason for marriage, but what are these complications. Being single is better. No accountability and no responsibility to anyone. I can focus on myself only."

"That is the problem; Love is not always the answer. Love marriage fails more than arrange marriage. You know many couples who seem to have a love marriage are arranged by themselves not by love but due to compatibility. Those marriages are more successful." Connells replies.

"More successful?" Harrell questions

Connells thought for a few seconds. "Hm… see, let's think about a relationship. A man and women will meet; they fall in love and then they start to know each other. They might test each other. If the relationship lasts, they will eventually get married. But statistically speaking it takes 3-5 years for these couples to get married.

After the wedding, when they sign the official marriage contract, a bond is formed. While they were free in their relationship, marriage binds them, and nobody enjoys being tied down. After about a year, they realize the idealized expectations of marriage can never be met, a truth that might also apply to you

Modern arranged marriages often begin with a careful, honest conversation between two people, who respectfully learn about each other's life, health, and dreams. Then they spent time to build a foundation of mutual respect and understanding, while they plan their wedding. The first years of marriage are a special journey of knowing each other more deeply and building trust. And when they grow to live with each other, some dissatisfaction and disappointment is eliminated by the arrival of their child. A delightful bonus which become their priority, which make them to forget their own personal desires and focus solely on their shared purpose, which is to build a happy family together. This somehow sure fire path to a successful marriage.

You know, people are much more straightforward these days. The divorce rate has gone up, and it seems nothing is working out. So, it might be better to be single."

Harrell said, "Single, it is better to be single. If I ask you, you have no other choice but to get married. Then which kind of person do you want to get married to. What is your type?"

"If I want to get married what kind of person she should be? I don't know. But I will definitely convince you to get married to me" Connells said.

"Really"

"Yep"

"Why?"

"I have met many people, but you are the one who let me speak my heart to you, you listen to me and talk to me without any filter. I know I don't know you completely. But I feel at ease with you."

"Ease, what kind of ease Sir?"

"Comforting Madam… Now let's go, we've walked out of Pallena" Connells escorts Harrell to her house and heads back toward his own home.

Harrell enters to find Liam and Maria waiting for her in the bakery.

"Where were you, I saw you leaving the church before us" Liam asks.

"I ended up walking in the wrong direction with Connell by mistake." Harrell replied.

"Hmm, by mistake, did you listen Maria, by mistake"

"Where is everyone?"

Maria says "Everyone was tired so they are resting now. Why don't you get fresh? I will make some tea."

"Thank you dear. Liam, why don't you try to do something useful?" Harrell goes to her room. After a while, Maria brought Harrell a couple of cups of tea while she was resting in her room.

"What happen? I know Jade doesn't affect you that much. Why are you feeling so low?" Maria asks.

"How was today's Wedding, do you think Susanne and Victor will remain happy ever after?" Harrell asks.

"No one can live happy ever after. But I can see that Susanne and Victor make things work out. They seem to be in love?"

"Today, the wedding happens not because of love but a threat that led to an adjustment.

Victor got Susanne pregnant. When she asks him to take responsibility, he refused and tried to run away, then Susanne went to his house and asked his parent to make him understand that if Victor do not agree then she might file a complaint against him. So, due to fear, they eventually agreed. Since she was pregnant already, they decided the date should as early as possible.

Now tell me how you think about today's wedding?" Harrell says.

"That's surprising. They looked so happy. How is Susanne holding up so well, is she really okay?" Maria asks while sitting in front of Harrell.

"I don't know about that, I was just asking her not to do this. She might regret this later. She said that Victor came to her just before the wedding and told Susanne that he apologized for this behaviour and is happy to take the responsibly to their child. Do you think he is changed or pretending to change?

Is he doing some kind of Drama, what if he tried to hurt Susanne?" Harrell says.

"Well, I didn't expect Susanne to be so strong and independent.

We need to be reasonable here. Susanne's family, the Stones, is quite powerful, and their law firm is very famous. She also has substantial assets, as she owns half the family estate. With the consistent protection of her Uncle, Brian, Susanne will always be safeguarded from harm.

They will never let anything bad happen to Susanne.

People do change, and we must hold onto the hope that she will have a bright future" Maria says

"Maria, I don't understand why she has to take such a decision. She is my friend, but I cannot forget the fact that she used fear, a threat to control Victor and made him marry her, against his will. Even though he agreed, why does she want to be with a guy who rejected her in the first place? Do women really change when they become pregnant? Is it about being strong or being harsh. A girl who was bubbly and careless suddenly becomes fearless and daring." Harrell, unfiltered thoughts burst in front of her sister-in-law Maria.

Maria says "When women make decisions, they are decisive and unshakable. Women are forced to take responsibility at an earlier age. Women tend to gain wisdom earlier in life than men.

Do you know when we first met you didn't like me?"

"Well, I am not going to deny that. I thought you forced yourself on my brother," Harrell replies.

"Yep, I knew you might be thinking that I forced myself on Liam and got us married. But the secret is "It is true". Maria says.

"You are joking right? My brother is not the kind of person to be pushed to such level. I thought you guys were in love." Harrell asks.

Maria says "4 year ago, I met you brother for the first time in the office of my Father.

My father is the Principal of the College, my mom is HOD of Psychology and I was teaching Business English. We are a disciplined family. I lived with the rules and was very comfortable with my lifestyle. I was getting a lot of praise in the College. Some used to say I am going to be the next Principal for sure.

Your brother Liam came to the college as Business Statistics and Mathematics' Professor. He took all the attention as being the perfect professor. He was very strict with students, and they are terribly scared of him. Well even now the situation is the same.

At that time, I had a boyfriend named John. John was very carefree; kind of 'opposites attract' situation. I loved him a lot. But my father hated him.

My father liked Liam a lot and one day he asked me to think of Liam as future husband. My father thought that Liam can be good Principal and can manage this college well in future.

And on the other hand, Liam was very rude to me. He never used to approach me. When he used to see me, he looked at me like I was some kind of whore or something, which made me hate him even more.

So, I went to my boyfriend, John and asked him about our future. My boyfriend said he wants us to go live in the capital and run some shop and do business. I found that very immature. I tried my level best to make him understand the reality and asked him to get a job first. On the last date, he asked me to wait for him before he left for the capital. It was 9 PM at night, I was standing outside the café, and I was sad and disappointed. Then some delinquents tried to approach me. I got scared. Before I could think of anything, I got pulled by someone. When I looked at that person, he was Liam. He asked them to go away but they were not ready to listen. Out of nowhere, Liam unexpectedly grabbed my hand, and we started running. We continued until we found a hiding spot. We remained there for a few minutes, and then your brother took me to his small apartment for that night.

He insisted that I take the bedroom while he slept in the hall. His kindness surprised me but at the same time impressed me. It made me feel completely safe. I slept peacefully that night, and my feelings for him started to evolve. However, every time I tried to reach out to him afterward, he never gave me the opportunity to talk.

So finally, I asked my father to approach him and ask for marriage. Liam agreed because he knew that if he agreed to get married to me, he would get a promotion for sure.

I liked him, he was very strict and stubborn, with lots of boundaries. When I came into this house for the first time as his fiance, I saw a different side of him; being mean to you, always bickering with you.

In front of everyone, he irritates his sister, but behind her back, he protects her at any cost. He is the son who ensure your mom live stress-free and pretend to joke around but behind he is serious about you guys. He doesn't want his family to go through any hardship.

You know, when news of your divorce came to us, he and I went to see Jade in Thown. After talking to Jade, knowing the reason behind your divorce, Liam punched him. His protective instinct toward his family is something I found incredibly sexy.

Our marriage was arranged by me, and he took a lot of time to love me back. He might be materialistic sometimes but once he takes responsibility, he earnestly fulfils it. When women are pregnant, they traditionally move to their mother's house. My choice is to stay here with you, Mom, and Liam because a child with his best qualities is something I really desire.

"You are the only one who can stand beside him. Seriously I am not joking. Only you can handle him." Harrell says

Maria says "Marriage, my dear, is like this. It's a sad reality when you can't be with the one you love. The truth is, you should marry someone you can bear understand, tolerate, and share responsibilities with.

Your friend must be shaken up right. But she is putting up with this situation, because she wants to have a child and husband who is the father of her child. It is tough but many marriages happen due to fear and force, then people cave in and find their own happiness. I mean, they create their happiness.

Especially Women in this world get married because of fear. Fear of society, fear of loneliness' and fear of never been protected.

You know that "Everything is fair in Love and War." War and Love are always compared. But have you ever wondered that Love is not the opposite of War, it is peace.

Every person involved in war desire peace. If one cannot find peace in their misery, they will initiate a War to have desired peace. There is no guarantee if one will ever receive their desired outcome, even though they still fight for it. As the time goes on, people eventually settle down thinking whatever they have is enough for them and they should be happy rather than wasting time in worrying.

You loved Jade, right? But did it workout?"

Harrell says, "No".

Maria says, "Then, love is not main reason for marriage to be successful. Love is not Life. Life is more than that. I know you understand what I talking about."

Harrell says, "Yes, I understand, Life is much more than finding a person who you truly love."

Maria stands and walks toward the open window. She leans toward the window and takes a deep breath. She looks at Harrell and says, "Since I spoke about love and peace, there's something about war you need to understand. War is everywhere: inside your mind, between friends, between enemies, and between strangers."

Everyone is fighting to have better life. Everyone is trying their hardest.

Harrell, take this advice from me seriously. Try to become opportunist."

Harrell asked, "Opportunist, why?"

"Because I can see you can have something great right in front of you. But you as a honest person is just trying to have something good, even though in back of your mind you know that you can have greater.

You aren't doing anything wrong. But can you be more observant and try to look around. See and grab what is being offered to you before it will walk away. What can be useful and beneficial to you? Try to differentiate your options and opportunities, grab the one which have more guarantees."

I am just saying Dr. Connells is great guy; he is a Doctor in the City hospital. He has a secure job. He seems to be interested in you. There are a lot of girls trying too hard for him, I saw in the wedding today. If you wait for your feeling to grow for him, he might mingle with some other girl.

It's your life not mine. You are capable to make decision for yourself. But don't be left behind. You never know, maybe next time, you might be attending Dr. Connells wedding." Maria says while putting her hair behind her ears.

Harrell says "Maria, should I tell you secret."

"Sure"

"I will be the one who will marry Connells."

Maria smiles and asks, "Really?"

Harrell says, "Yes, I come to known, I give him comfort and I realised he tries to keep me safe. Before other girl tries, I will put in the efforts so that instead of just calling me a person who puts him at ease, he will say that he has become habituated to me. I have my ugly side too. I cannot lose this time. Instead of finding love, I believe I have started to walk in the path to fulfil my selfish desire. Connells is person who brings me to peace. In this rush of world, he is slowly becoming my desire."

Maria smirks, "Well, that sounds good. **Isn't it the Peace, that everyone chooses in the end?**"

Chapter 10 +1

You can reclaim your power only when you can stare at your fear

"Something's wrong"

Debbie asks her son Connells, who is sitting in the living room with his hands empty, no glass of wine beside him.

"Nothing, just thinking" Connells says.

"Thinking, you father used to think like this in middle of the night" Debbie says, as she takes a seat beside Connells.

The room was quiet; only the golden light from the night lamp and the silver moonlight from the window took turns illuminating the space.

The silence breaks with a simple question of Connells "Mom, do you feel lonely, when I go to work. Will you never come and live with me in Watsar?

"I can, but my heart doesn't want to leave this place." Debbie says, tilting her head onto Connells' shoulder.

"Is it comfy here?" Connells asked.

"Yes" Debbie answers, "I can see you are getting popular these days, especially with girls."

"I am not the one who they like, they only like my profession." Connells replies.

Debbie asks with concern "Is it because of…"

"No, I do not care anymore about them; I understood that Woman can be quite materialistic sometimes. Not everyone is like you." Connells says.

"I wish only happiness for you, son. Can't you give yourself one more chance? You might someone you will love." Debbie.

"One more chance? I believe in arrange marriages now, why don't you find some girl for me, who is willing to live with you in this village and is good in all household work." Connells says

"I am little disappointed; I want you to have a life partner and I want a daughter not a maid." Debbie asks.

"Wow, I will bring some medal from Watsar next time" Connells replies

There is a knock on the door. Connells sees the clock, it is 11:30 PM. Connells walks toward the door and ask "Who is it?"

"It's me, Harrell" Harrell replies

Connells open the Door and see Harrell with a basket and pot. "Sorry for the late, there were left over from today's wedding party. Grandma asked me to share some with friends; I gave some to Vivi, Sara, Laurence, Juliana, and Joana. But still there were leftovers. So, I thought of you, so I brought some for you and Debbie" Harrell says as she comes inside from Side door of Kimsons.

"No worries, dear, what are these?" Debbie asks.

"This is some chocolate cupcakes as Connells like this when he tasted last time and this is roasted chicken. I have reheated this in oven just an hour ago, so just keep them in freeze for now." Harrell says while she keeps the two dishes in the table.

"You could have brought this tomorrow morning dear" Debbie asks while checking if the chicken is still warm.

Harrell replies "Yes, I can, but Connells is leaving to morning around 5, rights? So, I thought he can take some of this with him. He live alone there."

"Are you leaving tomorrow morning, son?" Debbie asks

"Yes, I have some urgent work. I forget to tell you, in the rush of the wedding." Connells replies.

"Okay then bye good night. Tell me if any need help Debbie, I am always around" Harrell says goodnight to the mother and son.

"Yes dear, thank you! Good night!" Debbie says after she looks like her son and ask "She knows but I don't".

"What?" Connells says.

"Harrell know a lot about you, but I don't" Debbie asks

"Not again Mom, you do this with every woman who becomes friendly with me. She is good person and very reliable." Connells says

Connells goes to his bedroom, while his mom follows him. Before Connells can close the door, Debbie comes inside and starts listing the future dreams she has for this son. Connells stop her by saying "I know she is awesome, but I am not. So please, can you stop? She deserves to be with someone who can keep pace with her. She is dynamic and I am slow. I like sleeps she like dreams."

Debbie understands her son, she puts her hands on and makes Connells sit on this bed, "Is it because Sara called you Pathetic, do you really think you bore people. Then why do people come to you."

Connells replies, "Because I am just a doctor, they want treatment."

"Dear, can you ever try to listen to me? You need to look around. Your past is your past, but it cannot define you. Seriously, I will never be going to bring food for my friend this late in night, since I am woman. When somebody is trying to put effort for you, you need to acknowledge them. Don't let people down." Debbie trying to make her son understands, though she has tried millions of times.

"Harrell is smart woman who is successful and spontaneous. She is good looking and won't settle with me" Connells says

"She does not want, have you ever asked her out? Veronica and I are very old friends. Can't you even try, just for me? I want to see you married before I die." Debbie asks her son desperately.

Connells stand and make her mom sit on the bed while he sits on the carpet "Listen, I am not saying I don't like her. But I don't want to live with someone or share a room. I am tired of this expectation and then disappointments. I am happy and comfortable with my life. No one interferes, no one expects, and no one get sad."

Debbie looks at her son and says, "Are you afraid of change? Or are you afraid of getting hurt?

"Mom, I kind of made a mistake and I am embarrassed. I think I basically asked her out without actually asking. I said something like, 'If I want to get married, I'll convince her" Connells say.

"You're much more forward than was expected. This discussion was about marriage, not just dating?" Debbie sarcastically comments and makes fun of Connells. Connells tries to stop her, "Good night mom, you can go sleep. Can you leave please?"

One person's embarrassing memories were another person's precious moments. Here Connells was trying to normalize things and here Harrell started to weave her new romance.

"A small push can create a landslide. In Panella, the disaster of attraction and interest is complicated by a fear of vulnerability and a hurtful history. The question is whether this disaster will turn into the beginning of something beautiful.

Connells and Harrell were two adults who started to like each other. Just as seeds need time to grow into colourful plants and flowers, meaningful relationships also require a significant investment of time. In our hurried world, that time is a rare commodity. Consequently, what once coexisted—a person's career, job, and love life—has become a set of difficult choices.

If you need quality of life, then disregard the quantity of time and work hard to achieve your professional and financial aims. This requires nothing more than one person's determination and intelligence.

For a personal relationship to work, it requires two people with two different minds. One person might be thinking about yellow, which does not mean the other is thinking the same. The other person might be thinking about blue. How, then, can a yellow mind and a blue mind create a relationship? It can be created through the quantity and quality of effort and trust. When a yellow mind works with a blue mind, they can blend their unique perspectives to create countless shades of green, a spectrum as vast and beautiful as the stars in the sky, too many to count.

When Harrell and Connells meet alone, there is an undeniable awkwardness between them. However, in public, they find comfort in each other's presence. Even people around them have started to notice the little sparks between them, and it seems their attraction is becoming obvious.

Will there be a little push or will this feeling will fade away like farts in the air?

I am certain; there is always a push. People like to interfere; everyone feels a need to control including the lives of others.

Mothers inherently want the best for their children. When there is a mother, there is always an act of interference.

"So, tell me, what do you think?" Veronica asks Debbie.

"I am delighted dear; they are always looking at each other. And I can sense Connells has an ultra-soft corner for Harrell." Debbie replies.

"Do you think we should do something? I mean Harrell really hates it if I try to tell her to do something. But she will do the same thing if I somehow signal her, instead of telling." Veronica says

"Listen, I was thinking, if Harrell can ask Connells for dinner. He might agree. He is shy, you know, right? Debbie asks.

"Really?"

"Yes, he is really shy?" Debbie says after she realizes the voice behind him is of Connells itself.

Connells replies, "I am really sorry Harrell, my mom is really worried about me, so she will be going to ask you to ask me out."

"Son, I was…" Debbie is cut-off by her son with raged eyes.

"I can take care of my life. Have you ever listened to me, then why should I listen to you?" Connells complain.

Harrell interrupt the conversation with a very strict military voice, "Connells, I was going to ask you out—maybe in the future when you might be ready. But judging by your expression, it seems you don't like the idea of us as a couple"

A silence of intimidation, inconclusiveness and shock can be seen in the face of Connells, Debbie and Veronica. Something is going to get burnt for sure.

"No, it's not like, I don't like you" Connells says, as word are whispered in his ear "Wrong words" by their mothers.

"I mean, I really like you, but I am not sure if this will ever be going to work out or not." Connells tries second attempt.

Harrell says "I am not stupid; I can tell you are interested in me. I wonder why it is so hard for you to say it. I cannot be with the Man who does not have guts to say it on my face. Also, I am not stupid either to just waste my time waiting for you to confess."

"You said, "I am not stupid" 2 times" Veronica interrupts.

Harrell continues, "So, listen carefully Dr Connells, I am really interested in you, and I like you as a person and you are not that unattractive. But I cannot dare to Date.

I have never seen anyone who is charming & hilarious at the same time. You are precious. You were never married, but I am divorced. So, the decision is yours not mine."

It was a bold move, but Harrell is not the same old person. Connells seems flustered & Veronica seems proud.

Connells sigh, "Harrell, I need to be honest with you about my feelings. While I truly appreciate having you in my life, I'm not confident we can make a romantic relationship work.

Our lives are currently on very different tracks. You're building a successful business that demands your full attention, and my job as a doctor requires me to travel for long stretches—sometimes up to six or seven months with limited communication.

What you're looking for right now is different from my goal of finding a long-term, marriage-oriented partner. I don't want to waste your time with something that might not develop into what we both want. I worry that these long periods apart would make it impossible for a relationship to grow. I'd hate for us to lose our friendship trying to force something that might not be right for us at this point. There are big chances that this love might not bloom. What if it didn't work out? Then how will we talk, how will our mothers can be friends. It will be all messed up."

Harrell says, "Really! You are scared, what if "us" will never work out. You really underestimate yourself, here take this" Harrell takes a small pouch of plastic bag with a small fish and give to Connells. Connells with surprise face takes the pouch and asks "What is this?"

"Here, a gift from me. Keep this little fish with you and try to take care of this. And here take the fish bowl also." Harrell says.

"Why? It's not something I want" Connells says

Harrell says, "That is right; it is not something you want. Do you think it is easy for me express my feeling? I know this is not love but it doesn't mean I should lose the opportunity to have someone great like you in my life. I am not crazy, right?

I remember you saying that if you ever got the chance to get married, you would convince me. I know a lot has happened since then, and you might feel differently. Since you have not yet seen the confirmation that everything will going to work out, you want to step back because of certain risks. Or maybe the fear is holding you back, Dr Connells.

Are you afraid to act until all risk and failures will be removed. You need to understand that once all the risk is gone, whatsoever outcome will never be going to come."

Connells asked, "Listen, I understand what you are trying to say but why you are giving me this fish?"

Harrell says "I want you to take a sudden risk. When a fish grows in this small bowl, this will make you believe that everyone likes this fish, has the potential to grow in their natural state regardless of the external conditions. No matter how small the bowl is, the fish will definitely grow. Only if you try to care for this fish. How this bowl will look? It depends on you how you decorate and add thing which will make this fish comfortable. When you will raise this fish on your own, it makes you understand on how so much you can create and so much you can attract.

There are endless flows of possibilities we can create.

You are scared, but please do not underestimate who you are and who you can be."

Connells listen to the word coming out of Harrell.

Harrell continue "You are deeply cherished by people from our village. Not because you are doctor, but you are good guy."

Connells ask “Do you think I can take care of this fish? I don’t have time for this. I travel most of the time.”

“Yes, you can, everyone in this world is resilient.” Harrell replies. “I know **you can reclaim your power only when you can stare at your fear**”

Chapter 11

I felt sudden urge to do something or else I felt like I am going to lose.

"Like this moment, hearing the cricket noise, looking at this sky, every bit of my surrounding is making me at ease but I feeling like something is missing in me but I am not feeling empty. I am meeting different kind of people; still feel like I am all alone. I am not sad being, it's just that I feel like I can be happier than I am now. I know I have a lot of opportunity but inside I feel like all the doors are locked. And I cannot open them now."

"That why you want to date me. I am an open door for you"

"No, Connells, that's not I am saying. I just want you to open a door to me, I feel like this is the time I should confess my feeling to you. If you say no, I will move on. I am tired of waiting. I cannot live this anymore." Harrell says to Connells.

This is sudden for you right, readers Harrell and Connells are in love with each other in a shared fall.

The trust built between them was a silent, careful structure, understood in glances and quiet moments.

Their lips, filled with all the words that remained unsaid.

The warmth of his coat, a comfort on nights that had grown cold.

Their eyes, finding one another in the middle of a crowd, a private universe where only they existed.

Hands held for no reason other than need, an anchor in the shifting world.

The moment they finally spoke their feelings was a breaking point, a release of the unknown.

Standing on the threshold, each held the key. Yet, both were too afraid to open the door, for fear of what was waiting on the other side—the terrifying cost of a love they were desperate to protect

The time has been waiting patiently, but not anymore. A hunger has awakened for words of belonging. "You are mine", will she hear it from him?

Harrell and Connells are sitting on the table beside a small garden outside the Hospital. It is around midnight; the city is silent. They are some people in the hospital working. You can hear the footsteps, rusted metal wheels and the song sung by the night creature hiding among the bushes.

Connells says, "See, I am not denying my feelings for you. I always knew that you are the one for me"

Harrell says, "So, does this mean…."

"Relrel, come faster, Veronica is looking for you." Ron comes out and speaks.

“Let’s go” Harrell stood and walked inside the hospital.

As Ron, Harrell and Connells reaches to Veronica, “What happened?” Harrell asks to her mom.

“It’s a boy” Veronica says hugging Harrell.

“How’s Maria?” Harrell asks.

“She is fine, doctor said she needs rest, and the baby is fine too. He weighs 3.4 kg.” Liam says.

“That is great, Congratulation Liam” Connells says.

“Thank you, Connells, for the help, especially today, really appreciate you Man. I seriously got worried. Thank you so much for today”. Liam says

“No worries” Connells says.

It’s been eight months, finally Maria and Liam are now a parent to a cute baby boy. The Serene family has a new member now.

“My quarter is right across the street. Does any of you need to freshen up? You can come with me.” Connells ask the Serene Family member.

“Ron, why don’t you go with Connells?” Harrell asks.

“No, I want to stay here.” Ron replied.

“Don’t be a baby, Harrell, Ron you both go with Connells for now. I, Liam and David will stay here.” Veronica orders. After a minute of discussion, Harrell and Ron go with Connells to his quarter he is currently staying in.

Connells opens the front door and lights up the porch, "Sorry for the mess, please come inside."

"Wow, Nelnel, your house is big." Ron says as he receives a slight slap on his back.

"Call him Dr Connells, stupid." Harrell enters the house and sees piles of books on table, on the rack and other surfaces.

"I can smell something different."

"Like medicines, right?"

"Yes, Medicines."

"Great, welcome to the house of Doctor of Medicine."

"Really?" Harrell says.

As the two guests prepared to settle in, Connells gathered blankets for them. The cold of the Watsar night had set in, so he took to the living room fireplace, coaxing the wood into a warm, crackling blaze.

Connells pours some cups of tea and passes one cup of tea Harrell & asks, "Where is Ron?"

Harrell replies, "He got sleepy, so I asked him to sleep on your bed. Is that okay?"

"Why are even asking that? Aren't you cold? Do you need blanket?" Connells asks.

"No, this fire feels warmer." Harrell sips her tea.

“Night are very chilly in Watsar, so here the blanket has been kept for Madam Harrell”, Connells brings a red blanket and puts at the side of couch where Harrell is sitting.

“February almost ending but night is still cold, isn’t it?” Harrell says while she looks at the cracking firewood.

“Yes,” Connells said, settling onto the carpet with his back propped against the soft cushions of the couch.

The cracking fire cast a spell, the two friends sitting alone in the living room with dark blue carpet on the floor. The smell of wood is combining with the smell of dry leave corroding on the ground, creating cosy comforting sanctuary.

“Are you feeling awkward now?” Harrell asks

“No” Connells answers.

“Thank you so much for today”

“I would do the same for any friends and any one from Pallena” Connells replied, “And please stop saying thank you.”

“You are always like this” Harrell said with small giggle.

“What does this mean? Always like this.”

“You’re so helpful to others, but whenever someone thanks you, you get awkward and start talking like a pirate.”

Connells says “Like a pirate, have you met one?”

“No”

“How do you know?”

"Whatever"

"Listen"

"Hmm"

"About earlier, when you asked me to open the door," Connells talks about the Harrell confession.

"Hmm" Harrell drinks her tea while looking at the small pit of fire.

"I want to, but there is a problem." Connells said.

"What problem?" Harrell asks.

"I have a research project; I need to travel to a different country for 3 months. It might take much longer time than that." Connells says.

"When are you leaving?"

"Next week, I was going to tell you, but you were really busy with the new factory collaboration. So, I didn't get time"

"Are you going to live there and not come back?" Harrell asks

Connells replies, "No, I will definitely come back, I will continue to work here in this hospital. It is a government job, why would I leave this job?"

"Then, why is it a problem?" Harrell asks.

Connells smiles, "No, I just want you to know, it might change your mind?"

"Well, it might, it depends on your answer. I have asked you to date me twice and you haven't replied to my proposal yet. If you want me, then I am willing to wait for you. If you refuse and want more time and if I met a certain man, who is nice, good looking and want to be with me, I might give him a chance right?" Harrell says while putting her empty cup on the side table.

"Well, that sounds reasonable" Connells reply.

A silence was echoed in the living room; the scent of wood was getting stronger along with coldness outside the window. The cold wind slithers through the cracks of the window. The cold crisp air touches Harrell's skin, as she takes the blanket and covers herself up. Connells stand tries to cover the window with curtain. The wind's moan sound like a lonely song that sounds quite opposite to the cheerful cracking of the fire. The combination of two sounds creates melody that is offering a comforting embrace within.

"If I ask you to wait for me, will you wait?" Connells ask.

"Yes, I will." Harrell replies.

"Then please wait for me."

"I will".

Connells says "You know the smell of spring always makes people feel different emotions."

"What smell?" Harrell asks.

"During this time of the year, many leaves fall from its trees. The dry leaves that fall on the ground start to decompose. If you step outside, you can smell this weird comforting smell, caused by volatile organic compounds released by bacteria and fungi as they break down these leaves. Because the nights are foggy now, this smell becomes more intense. I call this smell the Earth sweet smell.

I believe due to this smell, people behave romantic. This smell makes people feel fresh." Connells explains.

"I never noticed it" Harrell tries to smell. "It smells like burning wood here. Should I try to go out and smell?"

"No, I just wanted to know. Is due to that smell you suddenly asked me out?" Connells ask.

"No, I never notice such things, but right now, I love this smell of wood." Harrell says.

"I am curious, why you suddenly said those to me? Connells asks.

Harrell says "To be honest, it was not planned at all?

I felt sudden urge to do something or else I felt like I am going to lose"

Chapter 12

Uplift yourself with me...

The porch light casts a lonely circle on the front yard; Harrell stands there wearing an oversized brown jacket. It's been nine months; Connells has still not returned from his medical research across the country. She find a paper clipping in the newspaper in the morning stating that Dr. Connells and his team have been successful in creating a new drug that can be used treat diabetes.

"The sooner you let go, the sooner the good thing will walk toward you. If you can crumble your old self, you can build a new version of yourself. That will make your life beautiful with every morning taking your breath away." Liam comes outside with a notebook.

Harrell look at Liam with stoic expression. To which Liam replies "That's what is written in Blythe's book" and he closes the book and holds it at in his side.

"He might come back soon, if he wants to" Liam says again.

"He will." Harrell replies

"Then, why you worried?" Liam asks

Harrell says, “My mind creates noises, but in the end, I know that everything will work out on its own. If I know I am not wrong but what if I am naïve. I know I should forget my past and shouldn’t think about the future which is a mystery. Everything that is present is here & now. Waiting is hard. It’s like every day; I have to come out of comfort zone. And I do, but still, at the end of the day, he is still not home.”

Liam puts his hand on Harrell head and says “What you’re doing is right Harrell. Look at you; you have made our small bakery into a small factory. This proves that you are going forward in the right direction. You are growing. And even if it doesn’t feel right. Take a deep breath and slow down, you don’t need to rush in life.

Come on, don’t be restless, and come inside, it’s getting cold.”

“Harrell, where are you?” Veronica asks from inside the house.

As she hears her mother’s voice, she goes inside. Liam looks around and follows her and locks the doors with a click.

The Lights slowly shut, and only remain the crickets, having a competition with each other creating their own concert. The songs echoed through the night till the bird decides to replace them. Now birds are singing with different vibe, welcoming the sun for the changes that people thrive for.

Harrell comes out of the house the next morning, with dark circles under her eyes and exhaustion written all over her face.

"Seriously, when?" Harrell shouts.

Harrell comes out of the car and walks toward the small factory she has created. She has been called due to some problem.

Jerry comes to Harrell and says, "Ma'am this way, the oven was working fine but, in the afternoon, we don't know what happened. Suddenly, it stopped working."

"Should we call an electrician Ma'am" Martha asks.

"No, let me check first, I worked with my dad for the last 20 years. There might be an issue with the fuse. Martha, get me a torch." Harrell says while she walks toward the Main meter box.

As Harrell was checking, a person with torch appears behind her.

"Can you show a little higher?"

The man moves his hand to show the upper side of the meter.

"See, the oven is fine, it just tripped" Harrell says and looks around. The man gives her a wooden ladle, with which she resets the fuse.

"Is the oven working now?" Harrell asks while going back and standing in front of the oven,

"See it working now. When was this dough placed here?"

Martha answers "It has been over 15 minutes Ma'am".

"Hmm... okay then now you guys carry on. I will be outside for now." Harrell says after ensuring everything is working in her small baking factory, the Serene Bakers.

As she walks outside, she still feels that someone is following her. She looks back and sees that it's Connells.

"Ma'am, at your service" Connells says to tease Harrell. "Are you angry at me?" Connells ask again.

"No, I am happy, but I have been expecting this from the last six months, and it was not happening, so, I am a little exhausted" Harrell says.

"Well, I was expecting, you would hit me" Connells says

"I might, if you had taken more time" Harrell says while hugging Connells.

The streetlight was out on the highway, the two were driving back to their village Pallena. As they enter the village, Connells feels something different, he looks carefully and says "Did the road grow in our Pallena".

"Huh, grew? They were made." Harrell replies.

After Connells parked the car in front of Harrell's house, the couple went inside. A couple of hours later, July, David, and Veronica emerged with the couple to say goodnight. Harrell then suggested that she and Connells go for a walk.

"Have you ever looked at that star, that bright one, over here" Connells points toward the star.

"Yes, I saw, why is it a special star?" Harrell asks.

Connells says "Yes, from this moment on, this star will be our special. See that star? It's flickering angrily right, and seems like the star is trying to say something."

"Really, what is the star saying, Dr Connells?" Harrell says,

"The star is asking you to look in your pocket" Connells says with goofy voice.

Harrell stops and starts looking at her pocket and she finds a ring in one pocket of her Jacket.

"A ring" Harrell says with excitement.

Connells smile and look straight at her eyes.

"If someone gives me a 48-hour ultimatum to me to bring a single change in my life, or else my life will end. Then I will think for 47 hours on how to bring the change in my life so that I can spend every morning, noon, evening and night with you." Connells proposed to Harrell.

Harrell replies "You know my answer."

The couple celebrated with a hug, and Harrell says, "You know Connells, a rooster is also called a cock, and females are called hen. When they have babies, they are called chick. But when we eat them, we call them Chickens."

Connells says, "Where are we going with this?"

Harrell adds "People don't do the same thing for Turkeys. They give special treatment to Chicken but not to turkeys. It is either male turkey or female turkey and just called a baby turkey as the baby turkey. And when we eat them, we call them just turkey.

Isn't life so unfair."

Connells says, "Well I can see you had an amazing time without me. Just for your knowledge, a male turkey is called Tom or gobbler, a female turkey is also called hen. A Baby turkey is also called a chick or Poult. The names for baby turkeys are interesting. A young male is known as a 'jake,' while a young female is a 'jenny'.

This means life can be fair too, right?

Harrell says "Jake and Jenny. You really know it all."

"Know it all, it's compliment right?" Connells says back to his lady.

It's been 2 years; Harrell and Connells have started living a quiet life there. Both are living with their problems along with each other's support, pacing their life with simplicity.

Harrell comes out of the bath in a hurry, changes into clothes and runs toward the kitchen. There she meets her husband Connells making the table for both.

"Sorry, I was late, I don't know why I woke up late" Harrell says while the couple share their morning meal with an artificial white Rose flower at the centre of the table.

"It's okay, you are not bound to make breakfast all the time, Madam" Connells words bring a small smile to this lady.

Life is going on at their pace. Sometimes Connells comes home with severe back pain. He doesn't have to specify as Madam Harrell has found her ways to help him.

"Oh my god, please don't, it's hurting".

"If I don't do this, then how will you feel relieved?"

Connells's Mom enters their bedroom, "Can you keep it down? Why are you both shouting in the middle of the day? Oh, is my oil helping."

"No" Connells replies.

"It does, Debbie, he just cannot accept the fact that his spondility will go away if I massage his back with your special oil" Harrell says.

"First of all, it is Spondylitis, and this oil is horribly smelly" Connells replies.

The pace of their life is defined by his spondylitis and her allergies. Sometimes Harrell has to work outside to ensure her baking factory is working smoothly. Everything requires effort, so Connells sometimes bring a flask of tea for her and a meal to share lunch with her in the factory.

Yes, in this gathering, amid their insecurities and vulnerabilities, the individuals chose to construct a bridge: one built upon transparency rather than honesty alone, respect prioritized above love, loyalty valuing more than trust, consideration outweighing mere kindness, and determination eclipsing reconciliation.

Today is the 25th anniversary of July and David's marriage, it is a surprise party planned by Harrell and Liam.

"July and David are coming from their date, hide now" Liam asked.

"We are already hiding; You're the one looking out from the window" Harrell says.

Liam goes to the corner of the chair and finds a familiar scent; he puts his hand there and realizes it's Connells, not Maria.

"Why you use the same perfume as Maria" Liam asks. Connells replies, "Huh? This is men's perfume, why would…"

"Shut up!! Both of you, they are coming." Vivi says.

"You can talk too" Liam asks.

"Liam, behave" Maria says.

"But she never talks to me. This is the first time I heard her voice. I thought she was deaf?" Liam says

"It's not deaf, it's called mute" Connells correct.

"You think you are smarter, I have doctorate, I am Dr Liam Serene. And you are just plural name, Nelnel" Liam argues.

"I am real doctor, not a fake like you" Connells replies.

"I will cut your finger; you won't be able to do surgery" Liam snaps.

"He doesn't do surgeries." Victor says.

"Huh!! Why?" Susanne asks

"He is Doctor of Medicines." Maria clarifies, "That's why?"

The doors open and July and David enter the living room.

"SURPRISE!!!! HAPPY MARRIAGE Anniversary" Pallena is having a lively night tonight, the powerful joy in their limitations can makes things comfortable for a group of people of different kinds.

The family has a hectic night party, but a peaceful evening cooking together.

Harrell sits beside Connells after dinner. As Harrell sneezes and Connells put a small stole on her.

In these moments, they were just two people in love, navigating the messy realities of life with a shared understanding that made their own burdens lighter. They had found not a cure, but a kind of healing-comfort knowing that "you are not alone."

"How you managed to stay together for so long?" Louise asked.

To which, July replies, "Well, we've come to understand something by observing other relationships. The paths each person walks are fundamentally different. David and I are moving forward, but at different paces, with different approaches on distinct journeys. We have our own limitations and strengths. However, there is a consistent reassurance, David always gives to me: 'No worries, you can **uplift yourself with me...**'"

Harrell ask "Should we name that star?"

Connells says, "Let's call it Samuel Flicker"